*"You're moving too just for me, Again,"
Amanda protested as he pulled her closer to
him on the couch.*

"Am I?" He shook his head. "I don't think so.
I've got the feeling if I give you too much time
to think, you'll run away from me."

"That's ridiculous. I'm a grown woman, and I
don't run away from men."

"I'm glad," he said, his voice deepening and
growing rough. "Do you know there are secrets
in your eyes?"

"What?" She was startled, uneasy. His fingers
tangled in her hair, turning her to face him.
Warily, she met his gaze, wondering what on
earth was happening to her will.

"Amazing eyes. So green. Even now, in an
almost dark room, they're green. It isn't fair for
you to have eyes so green."

She couldn't speak. The pleasure of his hands
moving in her hair stunned her.

"Damn those eyes," he breathed, then lowered
his mouth to hers.

Amanda felt a hot shiver of pure, raw need
ripple through her body at the touch of his
lips. He kissed her with utter absorption, as
if there were nothing in the world but the
two of them. His mouth seduced rather than
demanded, beguiled rather than forced. Never
in her life had she felt anything like this urgent
desire, and she could no more fight it than she
could stop breathing. . . .

## WHAT ARE *LOVESWEPT* ROMANCES?

They are stories of true romance and touching emotion. We believe those two very important ingredients are constants in our highly sensual and very believable stories in the *LOVESWEPT* line. Our goal is to give you, the reader, stories of consistently high quality that may sometimes make you laugh, sometimes make you cry, but are always fresh and creative and contain many delightful surprises within their pages.

Most romance fans read an enormous number of books. Those they truly love, they keep. Others may be traded with friends and soon forgotten. We hope that each *LOVESWEPT* romance will be a treasure—a "keeper." We will always try to publish

*LOVE STORIES YOU'LL NEVER FORGET*
*BY AUTHORS YOU'LL ALWAYS REMEMBER*

The Editors

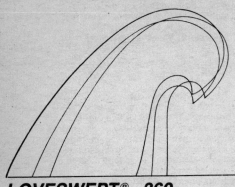

**LOVESWEPT® • 360**

# Kay Hooper
# Once Upon a Time . . .
# The Glass Shoe

 *BANTAM BOOKS*
*NEW YORK • TORONTO • LONDON • SYDNEY • AUCKLAND*

ONCE UPON A TIME . . . THE GLASS SHOE

*A Bantam Book / November 1989*

*LOVESWEPT® and the wave device are registered
trademarks of Bantam Books, a division of
Bantam Doubleday Dell Publishing Group, Inc.
Registered in U.S. Patent
and Trademark Office and elsewhere.*

*All rights reserved.
Copyright © 1989 by Kay Hooper.
Cover art copyright © 1989 by Ben Stahl.
No part of this book may be reproduced or transmitted
in any form or by any means, electronic or mechanical,
including photocopying, recording, or by any information
storage and retrieval system, without permission in
writing from the publisher.
For information address: Bantam Books.*

*If you would be interested in receiving protective vinyl
covers for your Loveswept books, please write to this address
for information:*

*Loveswept
Bantam Books
P.O. Box 985
Hicksville, NY 11802*

ISBN 0-553-22031-4

*Published simultaneously in the United States and Canada*

Bantam Books are published by Bantam Books, a division
of Bantam Doubleday Dell Publishing Group, Inc. Its trademark, consisting of the words "Bantam Books" and the
portrayal of a rooster, is Registered in U.S. Patent and
Trademark Office and in other countries. Marca Registrada.
Bantam Books, 666 Fifth Avenue, New York, New York 10103.

PRINTED IN THE UNITED STATES OF AMERICA

O      0 9 8 7 6 5 4 3 2 1

*For Jimmy and Myra*

# One

"This is the most absurd idea either of you has had. Ever." The only reason the statement wasn't wailed was that Amanda Wilderman hadn't been heard to wail since her infant days, some twenty-odd years before.

"It's an excellent idea," Amanda's seventeen-year-old cousin Samantha countered, "if only to get you out of your jeans and off your horses. Dammit, Manda, put your foot in!"

Amanda obeyed, but when she stepped into the other shoe and looked down at what was adorning her small, narrow feet, she really came close again to wailing. "You're out of your minds!"

Her other cousin, sixteen-year-old Leslie, giggled as she stood back, observing the effect of the costume Amanda wore. "This is going to be great!"

"It won't work," Amanda said, her voice taut as steel. "I've seen the guest list for this damned masquerade, and I know for a fact there are at least fifty women attending who can, and no doubt will, knock the socks off even so jaded a man as Mr. Ryder Duncan Foxx. So what makes you think *I'm* going to bowl him over?"

Samantha and Leslie exchanged glances, and the former said dryly, "Don't tell her; it'll only make her head swell."

Amanda gave both her cousins a disgusted look. "Funny. That's funny."

"Look, Manda," Sam said gravely but with a twinkle lurking in her eye, "you gave your word, remember? Any favor short of breaking the law, which this isn't. We've been collecting IOUs from you since last Christmas, and tonight's your night to pay up—in full."

If Amanda gnashed her teeth, at least it wasn't audible. "I should have known you two were up to something when you taught me to play poker. Why can't I just pay up in cash like any normal person?"

"Because we play for favors. You agreed."

"I agreed to too damned many things, it seems." Amanda frowned suddenly. "I have an awful hollow feeling in the pit of my stomach. Have you two been planning this for six months? No . . . not even you—"

"Guilty." Leslie grinned. "That's when the masquerade was announced."

In a reasonable tone Sam said, "Ryder Duncan Foxx is absolutely perfect for you, but you'd shy away in a minute if he knew who you were. This way he won't know anything about you. All he'll see is a mysterious, beautiful young woman who'll steal his heart."

Amanda made a sound. It was a choked little sound, a sound that was an odd mixture of anguish and horror. "You two aren't safe. You aren't *sane*. And I hereby revoke any deals made with you on the grounds of insanity. Yours. Not mine. Also on the grounds that neither of you is of legal age yet. God help the men of America when you *do* come of age, but that's their problem, not mine. Get me out of this costume."

Sam frowned. "No. A deal's a deal. Come on, Manda, what's one lousy night? You can leave on the stroke of midnight. In fact, we insist you leave *before* the stroke of midnight, otherwise it won't work."

"Otherwise it won't work," Amanda repeated dazedly. "I never realized that when I was reading fairy tales to you ten years ago they would corrupt you. Uncle Ed has to have you committed. Immediately."

Briskly Leslie said, "Manda, if you're so convinced it won't work, why are you protesting this much?"

Amanda pulled herself together. "You're right. Absolutely. What do I have to be upset about? I'm going to a costume ball, where I shall find at least a score of Cinderellas and an equal number of Prince Charmings. I shall dance and have my glass slippers trod upon. I shall drink champagne, and promptly flee before the stroke of midnight. The man you two demons have decided is my Prince Charming will never even know I was there."

Sam started to examine her fingernails. "Well, not exactly. Only one Prince Charming, you see. And only one Cinderella."

Amanda felt that hollow feeling again. "What?"

"Hmm," Les muttered, "we could hardly let anyone steal your limelight, could we? Ryder Duncan Foxx is coming as Prince Charming because he was asked to by the committee. Of course we couldn't have other Cinderellas there, so we booked up all the Cinderella costumes in town months ago."

"That," Amanda said, "must have cost you two a bundle."

Cheerfully Sam said, "Our allowance is in hock until the turn of the century anyway. Besides, one must expect a considerable cash outlay in any investment. You're ours."

"You sound like Uncle Ed." Amanda got a grip on herself again.

Samantha was pleased. "Thank you."

"Except that he's the sanest man I know." Amanda drew a deep breath. "Okay, fine. If your prince manages to find me in a crowd of two hundred people, he can have his dance—if he wants one—and I'll do my best to gladden your sweet little hearts and vivid imaginations. And that's all."

"He'll find you. You're going to make *an entrance*," Les intoned dramatically.

Amanda closed her eyes briefly. "I knew you were going to say something like that, you little monster." She was, by this time, resigned. Sighing, she said, "At least I can wear pink tonight."

"That's why we made you a blonde," Les explained. "With your red hair, you *never* wear pink. And everyone knows it. Honestly, Manda, nobody'll recognize you. Even your voice is different."

A little dryly Amanda said, "Because I've just gotten over a cold, and I'm still hoarse from coughing. Don't tell me you planned *that*."

"No," Les said, faintly dissatisfied. "We couldn't, of course. We were going to have you speak very softly, but this is a much better disguise."

"And the best disguise of all," Sam said, "is your contact lenses. We knew your spare set was tinted blue, so when you took the other set out to clean them last night, we—um—switched them."

Amanda sighed. "I wondered. Thought I was going nuts. So my eyes are now blue-green instead of merely green."

"Actually," Les said, "they'll look completely blue. The mask is black, so your eyes will look darker. And Ryder Duncan Foxx will find himself dancing with a blue-eyed blonde instead of a green-eyed redhead."

"Maybe he doesn't like blondes," Amanda suggested with a faintly hopeful air.

"Well, actually—" Leslie broke off with a yelp as Samantha kicked her.

"Actually, he loves blondes," Sam said.

Amanda eyed her cousins suspiciously. "*Actually,*" she said, "I wonder how you demons know that."

"We must be overusing the word," Samantha said innocently to her sister.

"Must be," Leslie agreed in a murmur, rubbing her abused shin.

Amanda clasped her hands together in front of her and glanced down at the spangled pink silk ball gown that was, in all fairness to her cousins, something straight out of a dream. Then she cleared her throat and spoke carefully.

"I really hate to burst your pretty bubble, kids, but

there are a few tiny elements missing from your plan."

"Such as?" Sam asked.

"Have you looked out a window lately? Surprise! We're in the twentieth century. Ryder Duncan Foxx is not, from all I've heard, a prince in search of his princess. In fact, I imagine anything out of a fairy tale would get pretty short notice from him; by all accounts, the man is quite firmly rooted in the logic of business. And, in case it escaped your attention, I don't believe in princes."

"We know." Samantha's voice was suddenly and unexpectedly soft, and her eyes were very bright. "You've had that knocked out of you."

Amanda was conscious of a lump in her throat. "Well, don't sound so unhappy about it, dammit," she said irritably. "I'm twenty-eight; if I haven't learned about the absence of princes by now, I should be locked in a padded cell."

Sam smiled. "Manda, you've been like our big sister our whole lives, and we love you. Tonight is our present to you. Tonight you're Cinderella. When the clock strikes midnight, Cinderella leaves the ball, as anonymous as she came. And tomorrow, when the society press does its bit about the latest charity affair, they won't have their usual paragraph about Miss Amanda Wilderman and how much money she has in the bank."

Amanda managed a smile. "It's a lovely present, Sam, Les. Thank you." She forced herself to keep quiet this time about her inevitable doubts.

"Just remember," Les said firmly, "you *must* leave before midnight. If you have to take your mask off, everything's ruined. We'll be waiting in the limousine out front at eleven forty-five."

"We wanted a pumpkin coach," Sam explained, "but we couldn't find one anywhere."

"But it is a *white* limousine," Les said with an air of having made the best of things.

"Where do I drop the glass slipper?" Amanda asked, chuckling.

"Anywhere you like," Sam murmured.

Amanda eyed her cousin but wasn't sure if she was supposed to take that seriously. She decided not to; it was just too absurd—even for Samantha.


Ryder Duncan Foxx had finally gotten accustomed to his costume, although he still thought it was damned silly. While dressing he had mentally composed a letter to the committee, in which he made it plain in blisteringly polite language that the next time they chose his costume, should there be a next time, he would inspect it before agreeing to wear it.

For tonight, however, he was stuck in this one. Prince Charming indeed! He didn't mind the paste-jewel crown so much, or even the short cape, but the glittering tunic could have used a few more inches; he was hardly ashamed of his legs, but encasing them in white tights wasn't his idea of suitable evening wear for a man of thirty-two.

He would have been more upset about it, but there were at least a score of other men in tights of varying colors, so he took comfort in the knowledge that he wasn't suffering alone.

Perfectly aware that he was considered one of the

five most eligible bachelors in the country, Ryder found the committee's choice of costume for him ironic in the extreme. Since most of his energy had been channeled into his business these past ten years, he hadn't had time or energy for being charming. And he had yet to encounter a woman who sparked in him even the faintest inclination to slay dragons or foil the evil spell of some demented witch.

Or the modern version of either, whatever that might prove to be.

Still, it was amusing to play the part, complete with royal dignity and princely bows, and somewhat surprising to discover he was really quite good at it.

The committee had pulled out all the stops. Thomas Brewster's garden had been transformed with the aid of a temporary wooden floor and innumerable lanterns into a ballroom fit for any fairy tale. The weather had cooperated nicely, supplying a cool, dry autumn night complete with stars and a full moon. And the orchestra had apparently been given every suitable piece of romantic music for the occasion.

The guests, paying charity for the privilege, were dressed to the teeth and having a grand time.

As co-host for the evening along with Thomas Brewster, Ryder did his duty and, for the most part, enjoyed it. Everyone at the ball had learned to dance immediately after the first uncertain steps of childhood, so it was a pleasure to have such accomplished partners. A few mothers, hoping perhaps for something more lasting than a dance, steered their unmarried daughters his way, but Ryder, experienced, coped easily and with disinterested courtesy.

The ball began well. It was nine-thirty, and all the

guests had made their way down the marble steps to the dance floor in the garden. Stealing a break from dancing, Ryder was standing on the far side from the steps, watching the couples moving decorously and half listening to the music. Even as his brain registered from which musical this particular tune originated, he looked up toward the steps—and lost all interest in music.

Ryder was striding toward the steps before he consciously realized he was even moving, his eyes never leaving the delicate enchantress who was moving gracefully down the steps.

He didn't know why, not really. There was nothing logical about his reaction to her. He wasn't particularly susceptible to feminine beauty, so it wasn't that. And he had already danced with a number of ladies who were strikingly beautiful. Granted a moment to think about it, he would have admitted a preference for brunettes or, even more, for redheads. So his desire to go to her was somewhat baffling. Still, he felt no inclination to resist his own impulse.

He decided vaguely that the music must have gotten to him. Or maybe the absurd crown he wore.

She saw him, hesitated almost imperceptibly, and then continued toward him.

He reached the bottom of the steps first, and waited.

The ball gown she wore was a soft pink, the spangles on the full skirt catching and reflecting the light in a brilliant shower of stars. Above the skirt, pink silk molded her impossibly tiny waist and caressed the full curves of her perfect breasts. The neckline was off-the-shoulder and its standup lace trim framed the creamy flesh of her shoulders and throat. Her slender, graceful neck was bare of jewels and needed none; only diamond earrings glittered at her lobes. And the fragile silver webbing of a diamond tiara, like a crown, caged her golden hair in an upswept style that was the essence of femininity.

A black butterfly mask hid much of her face from him, but he could see the gleam of brilliant blue eyes, and below the mask the lips were delicate, curved in a secret, enigmatic smile.

He had already seen the glass slippers on her small feet, but he had needed no confirmation of who she was tonight. Cinderella.

Without a word Ryder offered his hand when she reached him, and he was oddly moved to feel her elegant fingers quiver in his gentle grasp. He lifted them to his lips, still silent, and then led her out onto the dance floor.

He was beginning to understand how Prince Charming had felt.

She went into his arms naturally, gracefully, and danced as though the music were a part of her. She seemed content to be silent, but Ryder was not. However, though it was highly unusual for him and not a little surprising, he found himself considering and rejecting various comments and questions before he voiced them. He was astonished to realize that he felt like a boy on his first date, tongue-tied and terrified of making a mistake.

"You dance well," he finally offered in a sincere but decidedly lame attempt to break the silence between them.

"Thank you." Her voice was husky, musical; the glance she sent upward held a laugh.

Ryder smiled. "Does it show so plainly?" he asked in mock resignation.

"Does what show?"

"My lost wits."

She laughed very softly. "I've noticed nothing missing. Perhaps you just mislaid them?"

"No, I'm afraid they're lost for good. After all, how often does a man find Cinderella in his arms? And I'm at a disadvantage too. You can hide behind your mask, but I'm not wearing one."

"You're one of the hosts."

"It's a stupid rule. Take off your mask," he urged her.

"Not until midnight."

Ryder thought about it, keeping step perfectly with the music without having to pay attention. "Cinderella ran away," he said finally. "I recall that distinctly. She left on the stroke of midnight, and the poor prince was desolate."

"It served him right," she said solemnly. "Princes always have things too easy."

"Dragons," he protested.

"The dragons always lose," she pointed out.

"Because princes are heroes."

"And usually not very bright," she said gently.

"On behalf of princes everywhere," Ryder said, "I resent that."

"I'm not surprised. But it's true. Think about it for a minute. Would *you* carry a glass shoe from house to house, having promised to marry whomever it fit?"

"She had very tiny feet," Ryder explained.

"A number of women have tiny feet. I wear a small size myself—and there must be a dozen women here tonight who could wear these glass shoes of mine."

He considered that. "You have a point. I'll admit that the prince might have found himself married to the village shrew. But it turned out all right."

"Yes. Happily ever after."

Ryder heard the rueful note in her voice, and his own tone became more serious. "So you believe Shakespeare more than fairy tales? 'Put not your trust in princes'?"

The music stopped just then, and she stepped back, then gave a slight curtsy. "Cinderella knew only one prince," she said lightly. "If she'd known a few more, she might have been more wary. Thank you very much for the dance, Mr. Foxx."

"Oh, no," he said, catching one of her hands and tucking it into the crook of his arm. "We aren't finished yet."

As he led her toward one of the garden paths, she protested, "You can't leave the dance floor. You're the host."

"I've done my duty. Now I plan to enjoy myself with a Cinderella who doesn't believe in princes."

Amanda was more than a little surprised, but she made no attempt to escape him. It appeared that she had indeed caught Ryder Foxx's interest—but not in the way that Sam and Les had hoped for. Of course, they hadn't expected Amanda's own bitterness to filter through Cinderella's masquerade.

At that moment, for the first time, Amanda decided simply to enjoy the evening . . . to be the innocent, trusting maiden she was supposed to be. Every woman should have the chance to be Cinderella for one night, she thought somewhat wistfully. Yes, every woman deserved the chance to possess a starry-eyed faith in princes and love and happy endings. What was wrong with that for just one night?

So, quite without being conscious of its existence, Amanda allowed the chip on her shoulder to fall away. She was Cinderella, walking beside a tall, dark, and handsome prince through a moonlit garden on a magic night when impossible things were possible.

"You're very quiet," he said as they strolled down the neat path of the formal garden.

"Now I've lost my wits," she murmured, and felt a dim astonishment at the shyness she heard in her voice. Shy? Amanda Wilderman?

They had reached the center of the garden, where wrought iron benches ringed a trilevel stone fountain. The gentle splash of the water was soothing, and the music from the dance floor no more than a soft counterpoint.

Amanda sat down, grateful to be off her feet; the custom-made shoes were comfortable, certainly, but since she usually scorned high heels, they were still a trial. She was too conscious of Ryder's closeness as he sat down beside her.

"Tell me who you are," he said quietly.

She looked at him. The moonlight stole color, but his face was revealed clearly, even starkly, by the light. It was a lean face, handsome by any standards. A wide, intelligent brow, high cheekbones, firm jaw. His striking pale gray eyes were colorless in the moonlight, but the unusual vividness of them still was obvious.

Amanda drew a short breath. "Tonight I'm Cinderella," she said.

"Who will you be tomorrow?"

"Someone else." She hesitated, then said, "That doesn't matter."

"But—"

"Please. I don't want it to matter."

"So you *are* hiding behind the mask?"

Amanda laughed softly. "Of course. I crashed the party."

It was a reasonable explanation. The guest list for this event had been decidedly exclusive. And it wouldn't be the first time that a gate-crasher had taken advantage of a masquerade.

"I won't tell anyone," he promised solemnly.

"A true gentleman. Thank you."

"If you remove your mask, that is."

She laughed again. "I take back the first part; gentlemen don't resort to blackmail."

"Don't let the costume fool you," he said. "I'm no gentleman." He captured one of her hands and held it against his thigh firmly. It trembled in his grasp, and the impulse to remove her mask himself died before he could make the attempt. His free hand had half lifted toward her, but he slowly lowered it again.

Hearing her soft sigh of relief, he said, "You wouldn't have stopped me."

"No. Either you believe in the magic or you don't."

"And you do?"

"Tonight I do."

After a long moment he said slowly, "All right. But promise me you won't leave at midnight."

Amanda hesitated, but he had left her an out. She wasn't going to leave *at* midnight. She was going to leave before. If, that is, she decided to finish her role the way it was written. So she gave him her word. "I won't leave at midnight." And before his keen brain could begin examining that for a loophole, she added dryly, "The coach won't turn into a pumpkin, the horses into mice—or my gown into rags."

"Your fairy godmother must believe in overtime."

"She has a union."

To her surprise, Amanda thoroughly enjoyed the next couple of hours. Ryder Foxx was a charming man with a highly developed sense of humor, and was willing—at least until midnight—to accept his role in a modern fairy tale. They walked in the garden and talked, discovering that they shared a number of opinions and beliefs as well a quick wit and a somewhat ironic way of looking at the world around them.

They also disagreed amiably on a number of topics, which was another step in getting to know each other.

"Snails," Ryder said when the subject of culinary preferences came up.

"Yuk," Amanda said.

"You should try them."

"I have. That's why I said yuk."

He chuckled. "Grasshoppers?"

"Don't tell me you've—"

"No. I just wondered if you had."

In an aggrieved tone she said, "If I don't like snails, what makes you think I'd like bugs?"

"Not even covered in chocolate?"

"Not even covered in gold."

"That," he said gravely, "seems to take care of gourmet delights. Shall we move on?"

"Please."

"Well then, let's hear your opinion on the state of the world."

"I'll tell if you'll tell," she said in a teasing tone.

He laughed again. "I get the feeling we agree. The world's going to hell, but with a little luck won't get there until the sun goes nova."

"That about sums it up. And if you want another pocket summation, I'm for space exploration, rainy days, fewer taxes, baby animals of all kinds, good books, museums, flowers left in gardens instead of stuck into vases, old movies, spicy food, and the poetry of Keats."

"And what are you against?"

"Snails and bugs being termed edible."

"I got that the first time," he said reprovingly, and the hand lightly holding her arm slipped down to warmly grasp her hand. "What else are you against?"

Amanda couldn't quite recapture her light tone. "Oh . . . music with words I can't understand. Cruelty. A social security system running out of money. Hunting anything that can't shoot back. Cheating at solitaire. War. People who don't signal before they turn."

His hand tightened on hers. "And princes?"

She was very conscious of the man walking beside her, aware that something was happening between them. It was unexpected, and she couldn't quite define it. She felt uncertain, a little breathless, oddly excited.

"No," she said finally. "I'm not against princes. I just don't believe in them. How can you be against something that doesn't exist?"

"You have to believe," he said slowly. "Somewhere inside you. Otherwise you wouldn't be here."

She drew a breath. "But I'm not myself tonight. I'm somebody else. And she believes in princes."

For a long silent moment Ryder walked beside her, wondering why her denial affected him so strongly. He grew curious then about who had destroyed her illusions so thoroughly, and why the very thought of someone doing that to her made anger rise in him. He felt oddly that she was somehow unreal herself, that she was wearing more than a mask as a disguise. And when he spoke at last, he was surprised at the words that emerged.

"Does she believe in love?"

"I suppose she does." Her voice was low, curiously tentative. "I suppose she has to. She's a . . . a piece of a story about love and princes. What else has she got to believe in? It's all she is."

He stopped walking suddenly and turned to face her, his hands lifting to her shoulders. "What if I want her to be more than that?" he asked quietly. "What if I need her to be a flesh and blood woman?"

Amanda had been the focus of a man's charm before, but it had been many years since she had been able to accept that charm at face value. Her illusions had begun crumbling before she had left her teens, when her first serious relationship had ended badly, and the years after that had done nothing to shore up fragile ideals.

She had tried not to become cynical, but had finally come to the conclusion that either she'd had enormous misfortune in the men she met, or else it truly was impossible to encounter one solitary individual who had no interest in her money.

Amanda Wilderman didn't believe in princes.

And yet here was a prince. A handsome, humorous, charming man who kept her on her toes with his sharp intelligence. And he hadn't the faintest idea who she was.

But then something happened that she hadn't anticipated. A very simple and natural thing, given a man and a woman virtually alone together in a moonlit garden. And now she didn't know how to answer his question.

"I warned you I wasn't a gentleman," he murmured.

Amanda might have anticipated the kiss, natural under the circumstances. But her reaction to it went far beyond anything she could have predicted. She'd been kissed before, and by some "gentlemen" for whom the art was their stock-in-trade; but she had never felt anything like what she felt when Ryder kissed her.

His lips were hard, warm; there was no attempt to gently seduce or charmingly sway. He was no supplicant. He kissed her as if she were his for the taking, as if there were no need for preliminaries between them.

A wave of pure raw heat swept over Amanda, as if

she'd stepped out of a cool room to stand under the blazing sun of a hot summer day. It was a shock at first, and her hands lifted to push at his shoulders. But before she could even try to escape, a second wave of pleasure shuddered through her. She was hardly aware of a soft sound purring in the back of her throat, and didn't realize that she had moved until she felt the heavy silk of his hair under her fingers and the hard strength of his arms around her.

Those sensations gave her the willpower—albeit, just barely enough—to push herself back from him and try to turn away. But he refused to release her completely, drawing her against him and holding her firmly.

"Let me go," she ordered him huskily, staring down at the arms around her waist. She could feel the hard strength of his body at her back, and fought desperately to ignore the weakness of her own.

He kissed the nape of her neck, and said somewhat thickly, "It must be the moonlight. Do you think that's it, Cinderella? Moon madness?"

"Definitely," she managed to say with a shaky laugh. Then she caught sight of the luminous dial of his watch, and a chill chased the last of the cobwebs from her mind.

Eleven-thirty.

Where had the time gone? Until that moment she had half made up her mind to end the farce at midnight. But she couldn't. When her mask came off, everything would change. Her own guard would go back up, because, of course, Ryder would change once he knew who she was. The unburdened pleasure of strangers would be gone.

She couldn't see it end, not like that.

"Now I know how the prince felt," Ryder said. "I could get obsessed about you."

Amanda felt a pang, and recognized it somewhat ruefully for what it was. She hadn't expected it to be painful to have awakened interest in a man from behind the anonymity of a mask.

"You've let the moonlight go to your head," she said. "And so have I."

"Does it matter?" he asked.

"I guess not." This time Amanda managed to pull completely away from him. It was time; she had to leave while she still had the willpower for it. But how could she distract him? She took a few steps to a handy bench and sat down, adding in a light tone, "You've also forgotten your manners."

"Have I? In what way?"

"You haven't offered me champagne," she said reprovingly.

He stood gazing down at her for a moment, then said, "More evidence of moon madness. Would you care for a glass of champagne, milady?"

"Very much. Thank you."

"And will you wait here for me?"

"I promised I wouldn't leave." She wasn't lying, after all, she reassured herself. She had promised not to leave at midnight. And she wouldn't.

"Good enough. I'll be right back."

Amanda sat perfectly still until he was lost to sight on the other side of the shrubbery. A glance around was enough for her to orient herself, and she offered silent thanks that she was familiar with the garden. She picked a path that would take her around the makeshift ballroom as quickly as possible, then removed the glass shoes, snatched up her skirts, and ran.

She held the shoes tightly in one hand, unwilling to drop them despite Samantha's gentle request to the contrary. Her only other thought was to get away as soon as possible, and she took a shortcut through the Brewster house that led straight to the front door, racing past a number of startled servants.

Some of them had been enroute to the ballroom with their hands full of various things. Amanda heard at least one crash from behind her and winced, but didn't stop.

She burst out the front door and caught a glimpse of the white limo waiting at the bottom of the steps. But before she could make good her escape, a very large and very old gentleman dressed all in white, like a Kentucky colonel, crossed her path.

They tangled unaccountably, and Amanda felt one of the shoes slip from her grasp.

"I *am* sorry," the old gentleman said in a gentle, apologetic baritone. "Did I hurt you?"

"No, of course not," she replied distractedly, then caught the sounds of approaching footsteps hurrying in her wake. Where was the shoe? Her skirt was so full she couldn't see—"

"Oh, *hell*," Amanda muttered, and fled. She raced down the steps and dove headfirst through the open door of the waiting limo.

•   •   •

The old gentleman, large, bulky, smilingly benign, chuckled softly as he gazed down at the delicate glass slipper.

"Now then," he murmured to himself.

And with a speed and silence astonishing for a man of his size and age, he faded back into the shadows.

# Two

"I see you dropped it," Samantha said.

Amanda sat up and stared at her cousins. They looked very solemn. No doubt, if she could have brought herself to look at the driver—who had lost no time in closing the door, getting behind the wheel, and driving away from the house—he would have looked solemn as well.

Amanda felt like an utter fool.

She didn't try to pick herself up from the floorboard. The position, she thought, was eminently suitable. She tossed the remaining shoe into Samantha's lap. "Here. If I ever see that thing again, I won't be responsible for what happens to it. Understand?"

Samantha certainly did understand, and swiftly hid the shoe away in her voluminous shoulder bag. "Didn't you enjoy the ball?" she asked guilelessly.

Gritting her teeth, Amanda said, "Oh, of course. I

even danced with your prince. Which means that all debts are now paid in full."

"But what happened?" Leslie asked.

"I dropped the damned shoe because somebody ran into me," Amanda muttered.

"That isn't what I meant, and you know it."

"Nothing happened," Amanda said. "I went, he saw, we danced. End of story."

Leslie was about to demand more details, but Samantha elbowed her surreptitiously and said in a soothing tone, "All right, Manda. All debts paid. But at least tell us if you had a good time."

After a moment Amanda said, "I enjoyed it very much. It was interesting to be somebody else." Then she cleared her throat strongly. "I don't know what possessed me to run like that. I should have just stayed and taken off the mask." She took it off then and frowned at it. "Anyway, it's over now, and that's that."

"Of course," Sam said.

A couple of hours later Leslie crept into her sister's room, and found Sam sprawled out on her bed wearing an overlarge football jersey and a grimace.

"In case I haven't mentioned it before," Leslie said, "stop kicking and elbowing me!"

"Then stop blurting out things when you shouldn't," her sister returned, unrepentant.

"I'll admit that it would have been a mistake to tell Manda that Ryder Foxx actually prefers redheads, but there was no reason for you to elbow me in the car."

"Manda didn't want to answer your questions, couldn't you see that? It was best to let it drop. For the time being, that is."

"I guess you're right."

Samantha grunted abstractedly, then said, "This is going to be more difficult than I thought."

"Why? You said that if Manda left the party still masked, it'd be a good sign."

"Yeah—and she dropped the shoe, which is another good sign."

"She said somebody ran into her."

Samantha gave her sister a superior look. "She wouldn't have dropped it if she hadn't wanted to. That was just an excuse. Trust me."

Leslie did trust Samantha. "Okay. So why is it going to be more difficult than you thought?"

Chewing on her thumbnail, Sam said, "Because Manda's so convinced that no man could possibly love her for herself. I hadn't realized how strongly she felt about it."

"Ryder Foxx doesn't know who she is," Leslie said.

In a suddenly practical manner Samantha said, "Yes, but I doubt he fell in love with her at the party; that would be just a bit too much to hope for. I'm sure he was *intrigued*, and he'll probably try to find out who bought the shoes and where the costume came from, but that isn't enough."

"I think it's too much," Les said with some feeling. "If he finds out we were behind this whole thing—"

"I told you not to worry about it. Everything's set up on the *contingency* that he does try to find out.

And anyway, we're going to keep them both so busy they won't have *time* to wonder about glass shoes or anything else."

"Plan B?"

"No. No, I think we're going to have to skip directly to plan C."

Since the following day was Saturday, Ryder didn't feel the need to go into his office. He often did work on weekends, but he also had an office set up in his house outside Boston. He was there on Saturday, but he wasn't working. He was standing at the window, gazing out at a colorful profusion of fall leaves and wondering how in hell a man of his age and experience could be so idiotic.

As if pulled by a lodestone, he turned his back to the view outside and stared at his desk, where the symbol representing his idiotic thoughts rested.

A shoe.

A *glass* shoe.

He still couldn't believe he'd picked the thing up, much less brought it home with him. Surely the woman didn't think he'd be so besotted by one dance and a bit of moonlight in a garden that he'd lose his reason?

She didn't *really* think he'd cling to his princely role like a moron and charge all over Boston and half the Northeast in search of one pair of dainty feet? Especially after she had mocked the very idea. And she certainly couldn't believe that a couple of hours of conversation—fascinating conversation—and one kiss—an admittedly fiery kiss—could inspire in him a devotion so complete that he'd overlook the transparent ploy to gain his attention?

And it was a ploy, of course. What else could it be? Mysterious Cinderella shows up, uninvited, according to her, dances with Prince Charming and walks with him in the moonlight, melts in his arms for one kiss—one admittedly fiery kiss—and then flees before midnight.

Leaving a glass slipper on the front steps.

Questioned, the parking valet for the ball had said Cinderella's coach was a white limo. The modern version of a pumpkin and six white mice, Ryder assumed. But, sorry, sir, the valet hadn't noticed the tag number or anything memorable about the driver. The butler had *not* admitted her, he claimed, and so had seen no invitation.

After that Ryder had given up, drawing a mental line at questioning his co-host or the other guests. He wasn't, he'd told himself, that far gone.

He kept expecting somebody to offer the punch line of the damned joke.

He'd had a few lures cast out to him in his time, some of which had been rather creative, but women tended to be far more straightforward these days. He couldn't believe that any woman would go to the trouble and expense of a costume and rented limo just to rouse his interest. It was absurd. It was ridiculous.

It was working.

"Idiot," he muttered aloud to himself in the empty room, and went to his desk. He picked up the shoe and examined it minutely, as if he hadn't done it before. Just a pump-style woman's shoe made of glass. Water cushions in the bottom, fashioned in clear plastic. There was no logo or label anywhere, nothing to indicate the maker's name or business location.

But from how many places could one rent—or buy—glass slippers?

Ryder went around the desk to his chair and sat down, placing the shoe to one side. He looked up the number of the costume shop where his infamous tights as well as the rest of the costume had been rented, and placed a call.

The shop was open and likely doing a brisk business in returning costumes after the masquerade. Ryder asked for the manager, then waited and silently repeated to himself that he wasn't being at all idiotic about this.

"Yes, sir?" the manager inquired politely.

Deciding not to identify himself, Ryder merely asked, "Do you rent Cinderella costumes?"

"Yes, sir. We have three in stock; they've just come back in today. If you'd like—"

"Are any of them missing the shoes?" He made the question as cool as possible.

The manager showed signs of losing his. "Shoes? No, sir. The costumes were returned just as they were picked up yesterday."

"So you have three pairs of glass shoes in stock?"

"Glass? Oh, no, sir. The ladies don't like glass. Dangerous, if I may say so. And too uncomfortable."

Ryder resisted the impulse to tell him about shatterproof glass and water cushions while he gazed at

THE GLASS SHOE • 29

what was definitely a glass shoe on his desk. "Cinder-ella wore glass slippers," he reminded the manager, trying not to laugh at his own absurdity in this.

Badly rattled by now, the manager said, "Well—um—we use fabric or leather shoes covered with sequins. They sparkle like glass." He seemed a bit aggrieved at the implied aspersion on the store's reasonable facsimile of a difficult concept, as if to say they'd done the best they could after all.

"I see." Ryder cleared his throat and kept his own voice brisk. Given any luck at all, the poor man wouldn't think he was dealing with someone with a foot fetish. "I assume your costumes were rented for the masquerade at Brewster House last night?"

"Most of our costumes were," the manager admitted.

Ryder dropped his voice to a confidential note. "The thing is, I believe one of my friends played a trick on me last night, and she was in a Cinderella costume. Do you understand?"

"Of course, sir," the manager replied, still clearly at sea over the matter.

"Good. Now, what I need to know is whether my friend rented her costume from you. So, if you could—"

"I'm sorry, sir."

Dear Lord, was he going to have to go there in person? With visions of bribes and the like dancing in his head, Ryder said, "Look, even if your records are confidential—"

"It is against company policy to make our records available to anyone, sir, but that isn't the problem in this case."

"Then what is?" Ryder demanded.

"The, uh, size of the young lady's deposit made it possible for one of our clerks to ignore procedure, sir. Since the amount covered replacement of the costumes if necessary, there was no need to, uh, take the young lady's name."

"A cash deposit?"

"Yes, sir."

*Quite* an investment, Ryder thought, and then suddenly realized what he'd been told. "Wait a minute. You mean *one* young lady rented all three Cinderella costumes?"

"Yes, sir."

"Do you remember what she looked like?"

The manager cleared his throat. "The circumstances made me notice her, sir. But I'm afraid I can't tell you much about her. It was a windy day; she wore a scarf over her hair, and a rather bulky coat. And sunglasses. And she, um, arrived in a limousine."

"A white one?"

"No. Black."

"Dammit," Ryder muttered.

"I beg your pardon, sir?"

"Nothing. When did she rent the costumes?"

"Months ago. Just after the ball was announced." Somewhat apologetically, as if it were a slur cast on himself, the manager added, "No one else had indicated interest in Cinderella so early, you see."

"The ball," Ryder said, "had a fairy-tale theme."

"Um, yes, sir. But it *was* early. And we had very few requests afterward. Today's women seem to resist that particular fairy tale."

THE GLASS SHOE • 31

"That's what you think."

"Sir?"

"Nothing. Well, thanks for your help."

"Yes, sir. Anytime."

Ryder cradled the receiver and then stared at the glass shoe on his desk. "Curiouser and curiouser," he murmured. Then, with a determined air, he consulted the Yellow Pages and made a list. He'd check the costume shops first, he decided. Then the shoe stores. Glass shoes were apparently rare beasts, and *somebody* had to own up to having made, rented, or sold a pair.

He shook his head at himself, and began calling.

In the heart of Boston a harried store manager looked up from a neatly typed list of instructions and gave his grinning assistant a somewhat wild-eyed glare. "Those Wilderman girls," he said definitely, "will be the death of me!"

"Wonder what they're up to?" the assistant mused.

"I don't know, and I don't want to know." The manager tore his list in half.

"Better not," the assistant offered. "He might call again."

The manager looked at the phone as if it might rear back and bite him any minute. He moaned. "Oh, Lord help me."

Amanda Wilderman spent the following week wishing she'd never committed the utter stupidity of reading fairy tales to her cousins when they were little girls. Because little girls, she decided grimly, grew into bigger girls with minds warped from fairy tales.

It was only small things at first. Subtle things. Her bookmark replaced by one displaying a frog and words to the effect that it was sometimes necessary to kiss a number of toads before discovering a prince. An illustrated volume of fairy tales left on her bed. A tape that just happened to be one of the filmed versions of *Cinderella* in the VCR playing as she entered the room.

But when a recent business publication with a full-color photo of Ryder Duncan Foxx on the cover just happened to find its way into her lingerie drawer, Amanda had had enough.

She knew her cousins too well to attempt to stop them. No, she decided, escape was the only possibility. Years of Samantha and Leslie's peculiar high jinks had taught her nothing if not that her cousins would weary of their new game and give up— eventually.

Besides, Amanda wanted to get away for her own sake. She caught herself thinking too often of moonlit gardens and tinkling fountains. And kisses. She caught herself wondering if he'd found the shoe, and tossing in her bed at night because even if he *had*, the man certainly hadn't been bewitched enough to launch some harebrained search. . . .

And, because of all this, she was feeling a bit wild when she burst into her uncle's study exactly one week after the cursed ball.

"I'm leaving," she announced.

Edward Wilderman looked up from his cluttered desk, surveyed his niece for a moment, then asked mildly, "Where are you going?"

"I don't know yet," she admitted, calming down.

"They're still inundating you with fairy tales?"

"You don't miss a thing, do you?"

"It's safer that way," he admitted.

"That damned masquerade," she muttered. "I'll never hear the end of it, at least until they've gotten it out of their systems. I have to get away."

He hesitated, then said, "Vacation, or do you want to be busy?"

Amanda dropped into one of the leather chairs before his desk. "I want to be busy. Say you have something for me to do, Uncle Ed."

He smiled at her, a man in his early forties with graying copper hair and bright green eyes. He had welcomed Amanda into his home when his brother and sister-in-law had been killed, had raised her and treated her as he had his own daughters. And he had been very glad of her presence and quiet strength when his wife had died five years before.

Now, gazing at Amanda across the desk, he wished he had some words of wisdom to offer her. There was a shell surrounding her now, one that hadn't been there ten years earlier and, he thought, would become unbreakable in time. It troubled him deeply to watch her fiery spirit become trapped in a cage.

Poor little rich girl. Amanda would be the first to mock herself. But Edward knew only too well that extreme wealth *was* a burden, especially to a young and beautiful woman.

But he might not have given in to Samantha's pleas even then, except that he had developed a somewhat rueful faith in his elder daughter's schemes. She had a disconcerting habit of pulling off the most unlikely strategies, and he never knew whether to laugh or be absolutely appalled. Leslie would no doubt have been horrified at how much their father knew, but Sam had always confided in him about her plans, however absurd they appeared to be, and he trusted—and prayed—she always would.

"Uncle Ed?"

He made up his mind. "Sorry, honey. I was wondering if you're up to this."

"Tell me, and we'll find out."

"All right. I mentioned that ranch in Wyoming?"

"The one you're trying to put in the black? Sure."

"Well, the repairs and remodeling have reached the point where I need someone on the spot to oversee the decorations, a manager, really. I'd planned to hire a decorator, but I'm a bit wary of whatever trend is currently popular, especially after that fiasco you had to straighten out for me at the inn last year."

Amanda smiled. "Starkly modern decorations *did* look a bit out of place in a Vermont inn."

Edward winced. "I'll say. And you did a beautiful job with that place, Amanda. Still, this ranch house will be a tough job. It could take months. You might even find yourself snowed in out there."

"I'll take lots of books," Amanda said.

"Thanks, honey, I really appreciate this. Now, do you want to be the boss's niece, or a professional there simply to do a job?" He wondered if he was laying it on too heavily; she wasn't a fool.

Amanda was thinking of how pleasant it had been to be someone else. "A professional, I think," she said slowly. "I'll use Mother's name. Since you had that duplicate identification fixed up for me, I'll have a driver's license, checkbook, and credit cards in the name of Trask."

"Good, that's fine. Now, we can go over a few things quickly, and then you can start packing. I do hope," he added politely, "that you aren't planning on catching the first westbound plane."

She grinned at him. "Monday will be soon enough —if, that is, you can keep Sam and Les away from me."

"I will do my poor best."

Amanda eyed him. "Uh-huh. Confess. You have a sneaking admiration for Sam's schemes."

"Admiration?" Edward thought about it for a moment, then said judiciously, "She absolutely terrifies me."

Samantha hung up the phone and stared at it as though it had become a very puzzling and contrary instrument.

"Well?" Leslie demanded.

Tucking a strand of copper hair behind one ear, Sam focused bemused green eyes on her sister. "I don't get it."

"You don't get what? That was Ryder Foxx's secretary you were talking to, wasn't it?"

"Yes."

"Well, where is he?"

"He is," Sam said slowly, "en route to Wyoming. Seems he's going to spend a couple of weeks or so out there on a ranch."

"Our ranch?"

Samantha nodded.

"Hey, you did it!" Les exclaimed.

"No. I didn't."

Leslie leaned back against the headboard of the bed and stared at her. "What d'you mean, you didn't?"

"I didn't send him out there. Les, I'd only just figured out a possible way to do it. But when I called to see if he was in today . . . well, he wasn't. He's already on his way to the ranch, and I didn't send him."

The sisters stared at each other for a long moment, and then Samantha smiled.

"Sort of makes you believe in fate, doesn't it?"

The Broken R Ranch was north of Casper, Wyoming, the ranch house proper located about fifty miles from the city. Amanda rented a car as soon as she arrived and set out for the ranch, mentally going over the information her uncle had provided for her. The Broken R had originally been part of the Patterson spread, a somewhat legendary ranch occupying hundreds of acres but known mostly for its rather eccentric family.

The last surviving member of that family, Helen Patterson, had moved out of the ranch house more than twenty-five years before, divided her land in half, and built a new house for herself nearby. She'd sold her old home but, Edward Wilderman had discovered, had kept an eye on the place.

Under new ownership the Broken R had managed to show an occasional profit as a dude ranch, but Edward's offer had been accepted with alacrity. No money had been spent on the place for more than a decade, which meant that Edward's renovation plans were extensive.

Amanda knew that most of the major structural repairs had been completed, but there was still enough to be done that Edward hadn't planned to officially welcome guests until mid-summer of the following year. But a half dozen guests had already made reservations when he took over the place, and all were scheduled to arrive in the next few days.

Edward Wilderman had explained the repairs by letter and offered to return deposits, but none had taken him up on it. It was a hardy breed, her uncle had said with a grin, who would choose to vacation in Wyoming on the edge of winter, so there was no need to disappoint them.

Amanda was pleasantly surprised to find the exterior of the house looking so inviting, but once she went inside, she discovered that fresh paint over new siding covered a multitude of sins.

It was a big, sprawling place, built more than fifty years before, when large families had been the norm. The central section was a square three-story-high structure of wood siding with a steeply pitched roof; two wings built of river rock stretched out behind it with an overgrown garden between them. Both wings boasted only one floor, but there were a considerable number of rooms in each.

Only the central section of the large ranch house was even habitable, the rest being made treacherous by ladders and lumber and a crew of busy carpenters. And even the central section was unfinished, a number of rooms bare and smelling strongly of paint or plaster. That meant Amanda and the skeleton staff of cook/housekeeper and a single maid had limited space to work with to meet the needs of the half dozen guests expected within the next few days.

Strictly speaking, it wasn't Amanda's job to help deal with the domestic chores, but since the workmen needed to make more progress before she could begin her own tasks, she was more than willing to help out. She paused only briefly after arriving to unpack just a few things before pitching in.

It wasn't until she was going over the list of guests in order to assign them rooms that she saw, with horrified eyes, the trick fate had played on her.

Halfway down the list with an arrival date of the following day was the name of Ryder Duncan Foxx.

"Miss Trask?"

Trying to gather her scattered thoughts, Amanda looked up as the cook/housekeeper approached. She conjured a smile. "Make it Amanda, Mrs. Elliot, will you?"

"Then I'm Penny."

"Penny it is. What's up?"

"I hate to bother you, since you're just settling in and all, but I was wondering about Nemo," Penny Elliot said, leaning against the high counter that served as a front desk. She smiled, her blue eyes pleasant. She was a middle-aged widow with a capable manner and an air of unruffled placidity.

"Nemo? Who's that?"

"Well, he—"

Before the housekeeper could explain, Amanda felt something cold and wet touch her ankle. She started in surprise and jumped back. There was a sudden heavy thud, and she looked down to find a very large dog sprawled bonelessly at her feet.

"What on earth?"

Penny leaned over the counter to look down. "Oh. That's Nemo. Don't worry, he's just fainted."

Amanda let that sink into her bemused mind for a moment while she studied the dog. He was a brindled black and tan mastiff and clearly weighed nearly two hundred pounds. While she watched, he stirred and sat up, blinking. He looked up at her, and his tail thumped against the floor. In his black-masked face, the heavy wrinkles around his big eyes made him look like a startled octogenarian, she thought.

She looked at Penny. "He fainted?"

"Well, yes. Whenever he's startled or scared, he faints. You must have startled him."

"I didn't know dogs fainted," Amanda said after considering the matter dispassionately.

"He's the only one I've ever known to do so. The vet in town says he's never seen it either. Anyway, that's why he washed out of the army; they were training him to be a guard dog, which obviously wasn't going to work."

"Obviously. So why've we got him?"

Penny rubbed her nose. "The former owners of

this place bought him about four years ago. When they cleared out last summer, they sort of forgot him. On purpose. He's an aloof dog, and doesn't take to many people. No meanness in him, though. I've been taking care of him, but I was wondering what Mr. Wilderman wants to do about him."

Amanda looked down into Nemo's big, mild eyes, then looked somewhat helplessly back at Penny. "Don't you want him?"

"He doesn't like me well enough. Since you came out here to manage the place—"

"Just until the renovations are complete," Amanda protested.

Penny smiled at her. "Well, you're the authority here for the time being. Your decision."

Amanda glanced at the dog again, then shook her head. "I'll get in touch with Mr. Wilderman later. In the meantime, just—well, just keep feeding Nemo, I guess."

"Okay. Which room do you want for our first arrival?"

"Um . . . we'll put him on the third floor in the room at the end of the hall."

Lifting an eyebrow, Penny said, "That's the coldest room in the house; the furnace people haven't figured out where it is yet, but there's a blockage in the system."

Briskly Amanda said, "Then have the maid, Sharon, put an extra blanket on his bed."

"You're the boss," Penny said, still a bit surprised.

When the housekeeper had gone, Amanda stared down at the list of guests and bit her lip. It wasn't, she told herself firmly, that she was trying to drive Ryder Foxx away. It was only that the room in question happened to be the farthest from her own second-floor bedroom.

She also told herself she was being an absolute fool about this. Ryder Foxx couldn't possible know she was here; these reservations had been made months earlier. Uncle Edward had simply forgotten to mention he was one of the guests. And, at any rate, Ryder wouldn't recognize her as the Cinderella from more than a week before.

If he even remembered that woman.

Still, Amanda couldn't help but feel defensive and decidedly unnerved. Even though the masquerade hadn't been her idea, she was conscious of an absurd sense of guilt. She argued with herself during the remainder of that day and well into the night, and her defensiveness won out over guilt. After all, she told herself, she'd feel like a total fool if she admitted to having been Cinderella—and he didn't even remember.

The next morning, edgy and a bit heavy-eyed after her sleepless night, she kept busy helping out wherever she was needed. She was somewhat hampered by the determined presence of Nemo, who had slept outside her bedroom door and now followed her every step.

"He likes you," Penny said.

Amanda nudged the dog out of her path with one knee while she struggled to position a ladder in the entrance hall. "He gets in my way," she said, but kept her voice even and casual; she'd discovered that brusque voices hurt Nemo's feelings, and watching him slink out of sight with his tail between his legs made her feel guilty.

Penny smiled at her, then went upstairs when Sharon called down to her in a harassed voice. Alone in the entrance hall except for her canine companion, Amanda propped the ladder against a wall and looked at it doubtfully. She wanted to examine the strip of molding across the top of the doorway leading into the den; the molding was an original part of the house, but she thought it looked peculiar where it was. If it could be taken down in one piece, undamaged, she had an idea that it would be perfect trim for the mantel she was having made for the den.

The thing was, Amanda strongly mistrusted ladders, and this one looked more than usually rickety. She started to call for someone to come and hold it for her, but the crew members were busy in other parts of the house and both Penny and Sharon had their hands full getting rooms ready for the guests. So, anchoring the ladder as firmly as she could, she cautiously climbed up the rungs.

She was slightly to the right of the doorway, and held the jamb with one hand while she leaned over carefully to examine the molding. She wasn't the slightest bit unbalanced, and the ladder held steady. Everything would have been fine if the front door hadn't banged open just then.

With all his concentration apparently fixed upward on the mistress he had adopted, Nemo was startled by the sound and collapsed into one of his peculiar faints. Unfortunately his massive body brushed against the base of the ladder as he went limp.

Amanda felt the ladder shift abruptly, and lost her balance. Things happened very quickly. She began to fall, and cried out in surprise. But instead of landing on the polished hardwood floor, she found herself caught and held in powerful arms that were like iron.

Even in her shock at the near accident she was conscious of a sense of fatalistic certainty, and looked numbly up into the shrewd gray eyes of Ryder Foxx.

# Three

---

"You scared him!" she snapped.

For a minute or so Ryder didn't respond to the puzzling accusation. He was struggling with another puzzle just then. He had acted out of pure instinct when he came into the hall to see this petite red-head on the point of tumbling off her ladder, but from the moment he caught her in his arms he'd been conscious of an odd sensation.

The sensation wasn't odd in itself; he'd certainly felt desire before. But the suddenness of the attraction he felt for this woman was very unusual in his experience and more than a little baffling. She was certainly a lovely woman, and he'd always been partial to redheads, but the jeans and bulky sweater she wore was hardly sexy attire. He couldn't understand why he felt so much so suddenly.

And aside from that, when she had first looked up at him, her bright green eyes had held the strangest expression he'd ever seen. For an instant he'd felt an urge to assure her that everything was all right because she'd looked curiously overcome, but then her expression had gone wary and her eyes had shown sparks of temper.

"Put me down," she muttered now, more than a suggestion of gritted teeth in her tone.

Instead of obeying the command, Ryder glanced at the dog stirring at his feet, and her earlier accusation sank in. "I scared him?"

"Yes, you scared him. Put me down!"

Ryder looked at her for a moment, enjoying the way she felt in his arms, then took his time putting her down. "You could have broken your neck," he told her, more than a little surprised at his own scolding tone. "Hasn't anyone ever taught you how to climb a ladder?"

"I was doing just fine," she snapped. "If you hadn't crashed through the door and scared Nemo, he wouldn't have bumped the ladder when he fainted."

"When he what?"

"Fainted." She glared up at him, daring him to comment.

Ryder glanced at the dog and decided not to say anything. "Oh. I didn't crash through the door; I nudged it with my suitcase and it flew open like something possessed. What kind of guest ranch is this anyway?"

"One that isn't ready for guests," she said with a certain amount of relish. "However, since you and a few others chose to disregard the warning about the renovations, you'll have to take the place as you find it."

He opened his mouth to retort that he hadn't received any information or warning at all, but she went on before he could speak.

"All meals will be served in the dining room down the hall there, and if you aren't on time, you're out of luck. No room service. The heat works, except when it doesn't, and you might have hot water for a shower, except when you won't. The only telephone is on the desk down here. The work crew has the undisputed right of way in this house for the duration, so if they say move, *do* it. Any questions?"

Ryder stared down at her. She stood squarely before him, hands on her hips, so belligerent that he found himself torn between amusement and exasperation.

"Yeah," he drawled finally. "Who the hell are you?"

Stiffly she said, "Amanda Trask. I'm managing the place until the renovations are complete."

"Am I allowed another question?" he asked politely.

Even more stiffly she said, "Ask away."

"Did the competition send you in here undercover to sabotage this place?" For a brief instant he thought she was going to laugh, but the gleam in her eye vanished quickly.

"No. I'm being honest, Mr. Foxx. I assume that's who you are."

"That's who I am," he admitted dryly.

"Fine. I just want you to know that if you expect to get first-class treatment here, come back next summer."

Ryder thought of a possibly very important and lucrative business deal, but that wasn't what decided him. He shrugged. "Understood. Where do I register?"

"This way," she said, turning toward the high counter near the stairs.

He followed her, and waited until she was behind the counter before saying gently, "You're welcome, by the way."

She looked at him for a moment, baffled, and then flushed slightly. "Thanks," she said somewhat ungraciously.

"I was just being heroic," he said in a modest tone.

Her uncomfortable look vanished as the glare returned. "It was your fault that I fell anyway," she said.

"I've already explained that, Miss Trask. Or may I call you Amanda?"

She opened an old-fashioned leatherbound register, and thrust it across the counter at him. "I'd rather you didn't. Sign."

"Yes, ma'am," he said, and signed.

"You'll have to carry your own bags," she added in a very sweet and polite tone. "No bellmen, I'm afraid. Your room's on the third floor; turn right at the top of the stairs, end of the hall. Number 304."

"You've been so kind," he said, closely matching her tone. She didn't unbend, but he was sure he saw her lips twitch.

"I'm afraid you've missed lunch," she told him with the same spurious apology. "Supper's at seven."

Ryder went to get his two bags where he'd dropped them at the door, then walked to the stairs. Hesitating at the bottom, he looked across at her. "Black tie?" he inquired gently.

"Come as you are," she replied in the same tone.

"But company manners, surely?"

"Do you have any?"

"I was about to ask you the same thing," he said.

She widened her eyes at him, mildly surprised. "Why, Mr. Foxx, I'm wearing my company manners now."

He bit back a laugh, keeping his expression one of polite inquiry. "Are you *sure* you weren't hired by the competition to drive guests away from the Broken R?"

Leaning an elbow on the desk, she contemplated him with a total lack of expression. "I'm sure. But if you find your bed short-sheeted, please remember that we have only one maid, and she's very young. Inexperienced."

"I'll keep that in mind, Miss Trask. Anything else you want to warn me about?"

"No, I don't think so. Just watch where you walk. I'd hate for you to put your foot through a rotten board or trip over something. The last thing the Broken R needs right now is a lawsuit."

Ryder contented himself with a nod and climbed the stairs, deciding that the honors had gone to Miss Amanda Trask in the first round. He had no idea why her attitude toward him was so bristly, but he intended to find out. Of course, she might well be hostile to everyone because of her normal temperament, but somehow he didn't think so.

Short of ordering him off the place, the lady had done her level best to get rid of him, and he wanted to know why. It was partly simple curiosity, but he was also all too aware of the fact that he was quite definitely attracted to that surly redheaded spitfire.

And he had caught more than one glimpse of a sense of humor in her, which appealed to him.

He'd have a few days before Cyrus Fortune arrived, according to the message he had gotten just before he left Boston, so there was time to find out what made Amanda Trask tick.

He found his room easily enough, and looked around with wry eyes. It looked fairly comfortable, he supposed, but it was certainly bare. The walls had been freshly painted, he could smell it, and there were absolutely no decorations. A double bed with a faded plaid spread, a nightstand with a single lamp, a dresser, and a chest made up the plain and somewhat battered furniture. A newly refinished hardwood floor sported two worn Navaho rugs, the tiny closet held half a dozen wire hangers, and the bathroom was missing a shower curtain.

It was also definitely chilly in both rooms.

He was not, Ryder decided, going to complain. About anything. He refused to give *Miss* Trask the satisfaction. He unpacked methodically and put his things away. He left only one item out, and eyed it as he changed into jeans and a bulky sweater.

What on earth had possessed him to bring the damned shoe along? He couldn't remember packing it, but wasn't surprised that he had. Nobody had ever defined an obsession as something rational, after all. He placed the shoe on the shelf inside the closet and shut the door firmly.

Enough of that. He was too far from Boston to continue his search for Cinderella even if he had a clue as to what steps he could take to find her. And, truth to tell, he realized with a faintly guilty feeling that his first encounter with Amanda Trask had pushed both fairy tales and business to the back of his mind.

Puzzling over his own apparently fickle nature, he left his room and went downstairs. The second floor landing provided a view down into the entrance hall, and he paused there as he heard voices from below. He leaned somewhat cautiously over the banister, and saw that Amanda was engaged in talking to another lady. Or, rather, she was engaged in being talked *at*.

The other lady was small, spare, and silver-haired. She appeared to be well past sixty. Beyond that rough estimate Ryder found it impossible to guess her age. She was in faded jeans and wore a thick fleece-lined jacket with scuffed western boots on her small feet. And she talked a mile a minute.

Amanda was leaning against the high counter as if she needed its support. Nemo was sitting at her side, and she petted the dog's massive head in a rhythmic manner as she listened to the older lady's rapid voice.

"They were dreadful people, my dear, just dreadful. Weren't willing to spend a dime on the place, and of course that's idiotic. I was *so* pleased when the new owner bought it and started fixing things up right away."

"Miss Patterson," Amanda said in the firm tone of someone who'd been trying to get a word in.

Helen Patterson laughed. "Oh, they call me Miss Nell around here, child. And you're Amanda? Such a lovely name. It means 'worthy of love,' you know. Or 'beloved.' It depends on which book you're looking it up in."

There was a faint frown between Amanda's delicate brows, and a somewhat dazed look in her eyes. Ryder felt a flicker of amusement as he realized that in "Miss Nell" Amanda had met her match.

Miss Nell took a few brisk steps to the doorway of the den and peered in, her expression birdlike. "Oh, good, you've left it the way it was. This was my favorite room, you see, and I feel a bit sentimental about it. But where's the mantel, child?"

Amanda blinked. "The—? Oh. I'm having a new one made, Miss Nell."

"But you won't change the fireplace?"

"No. We'll probably have to sandblast the bricks, but—"

Miss Nell tut-tutted disapprovingly. "You'll change the tone of the room if you do that. I always thought this was such a *warm* room, so cozy, especially with the bricks all smoky from so many nice fires. My father hauled those bricks in a wagon behind four mules and built the fireplace himself. Fifty years ago, it was. Goodness. I was just a girl."

Amanda cleared her throat. "Miss Nell—"

"There isn't much furniture," Helen noted critically as she continued to gaze into the den. "And that sofa looks quite lumpy. If you want my advice, child—"

This time it was Amanda who broke in firmly. "Miss Nell, the new furniture is coming only when the rooms are finished. We'll make do until then. That room still has to be painted, the floor refinished, and the fireplace cleaned up."

Helen pursed her lips. "I like it the way it is," she said, turning to eye Amanda severely.

In a cheerful tone Amanda said, "The new owner wants it fixed up." Before Helen could say anything about that, she went on in the same friendly voice. "You didn't ride over here, did you, Miss Nell? The wind's picking up and it must be nearly freezing outside. Why don't I have one of the men drive you back home?"

"It's only three miles or so, child; I'll be fine. Heavens, I've spent days in the saddle in my time. Don't worry about me." She was moving toward the door as she spoke, briskly drawing on a pair of suede gloves. "You just give me a call if you need anything. Anything at all. I'm a good neighbor; anyone will tell you that."

"Thank you, Miss Nell," Amanda murmured.

As soon as the door closed behind Helen, Amanda heard an uncertain laugh escape her. Uncle Edward, she acknowledged silently, hadn't exaggerated; Miss Nell Patterson quite definitely kept an eye on her former home. She'd blown through the door like a miniature storm, bent on finding out exactly what had been done to the place and offering innumerable criticisms and suggestions.

Under different conditions, Amanda would have enjoyed Miss Nell, since eccentric personalities appealed to her. But Ryder Foxx had shaken her off balance and she was having a difficult time regaining it. She was feeling more than a little daunted. Carpenters everywhere, a big dog constantly at her heels with an unnerving habit of fainting, a strong-minded neighbor with definite opinions about this place and no hesitation in expressing herself, five more guests due to arrive in the coming days, and— and—Ryder Duncan Foxx.

Amanda muttered to herself, relieving her feelings with a few colorful words and phrases since she thought herself alone. But she wasn't alone, and the sound of a low laugh made her look up quickly toward the second-floor landing.

"Not very ladylike," Ryder said mockingly.

She watched him come down the stairs, wondering what she had ever done to the fates that they'd do this to her in revenge. The man looked indecently handsome in his casual clothing, she thought, the jeans too form-fitting for her peace of mind and the thick, dark blue sweater setting off the powerful width of his shoulders.

"Didn't your mother ever teach you not to eavesdrop?"

"Certainly she did," he returned promptly, a disquieting gleam of enjoyment in his eye. "I even paid attention to the lessons. I wasn't eavesdropping, Miss Trask, I simply didn't want to intrude. *Who* is Miss Nell?"

"She used to own this place," Amanda replied, watching him guardedly as he reached the bottom of the stairs and came toward her. "I hope you find your room . . . satisfactory," she added politely.

"You hope nothing of the kind," he told her in a pleasant tone. "Tell me, Miss Trask, are you this hostile to everyone, or do I deserve your special attention for some reason?"

"Some people," she said in a freezing voice, "simply don't hit it off."

"But there's usually a reason," he said with a slow, fallen-angel kind of smile. "I'm curious about that. Do I remind you of a discarded lover, is that it?"

She had the uneasy feeling that she wouldn't like where he was going with this conversation. "I have work to do."

"And you think I might interfere with your work?"

A wise little voice in Amanda's head told her that if she'd only keep her mouth shut, Ryder Foxx would rapidly tire of the sparring and leave her in peace. But she wasn't very surprised to find herself ignoring the voice.

"Mr. Foxx, the staff here—such as it is—has no time to provide entertainment for you. There's a grimy deck of cards around here somewhere if you want to play solitaire. There are horses out in the corral if you ride, but please leave a trail of bread crumbs so none of us is forced to disrupt the work by having to go look for you."

"You have quite a chip on your shoulder. I wonder why," he said thoughtfully, that gleam of enjoyment still present in his eye. "It might be worth my while to find out."

Amanda felt a definite shock. She recognized that speculative tone in his voice, and it shook her. Totally against her will, she felt a rush of heat from somewhere inside her, and her legs went weak.

No, she thought blankly. Oh, no . . .

She squared her shoulders and glared at him. "I have a job to do here. So whatever you've got in mind, you can forget it."

No more than a couple of feet away from her, he leaned an elbow on the counter and looked her over quite deliberately from her running shoes to her bright red hair. "Didn't *your* mother ever teach you not to throw down a gauntlet?" he drawled.

Amanda fought a sensation of half-excited panic. The only effect her rudeness seemed to have on him was to encourage him even more, and she didn't know what to do about it. She couldn't deceive herself into believing that she didn't enjoy the sparring, but she was too conscious of this man to allow any kind of relationship to develop—even an argumentative one. Particularly when all her instincts told her that getting involved with him on any level would be like striking a match in a room full of explosives.

She got a grip on herself. "Any gauntlet you see is imaginary, Mr. Foxx."

"Is it? Well, we'll find out soon enough, won't we, Miss Trask? In the meantime don't let me keep you from your work."

Amanda managed to keep her face expressionless as she turned away from the counter and headed down the hall toward the south wing of the house, but it was difficult. She felt definitely bested in the encounter, and found her thoughts divided between wry amusement and panicked bewilderment.

Her sense of responsibility made it impossible for her to call her uncle and ask him to find someone else for the job, and that meant she was stuck for the duration. And she was uneasily aware that her hostility toward Ryder Foxx had done nothing except pique his interest.

The man had been at the ranch less than two hours, and already her nerves were on edge. She told herself that her only option was to ignore him as much as possible and keep herself busy, to stay out of his way. It was good advice. She only hoped that she could take it.

· · ·

"You missed supper, Miss Trask."

Amanda felt herself tense. So much for good advice, she thought wryly. She'd managed to keep out of Ryder's way for several hours, surrounding herself with the work crew while they were there, then retreating into the den with paperwork. She'd built a fire in the old fireplace to combat the chill of the room, and was curled up at one end of the couch looking over furniture catalogues.

Nemo, her constant companion, was sprawled out on the frayed hearth rug snoring softly.

She watched as Ryder came around the end of the couch and sat down, annoyed with herself because she couldn't help thinking that he moved with a cat's unconscious grace.

"Am I interrupting?" he asked innocently.

"Yes," she said.

"You can't work all the time. It's bad for your health, to say nothing of your temper."

"Mr. Foxx—"

"Ryder," he suggested.

Enough, Amanda decided, was enough. She looked him straight in the eye. "Why don't we save ourselves a lot of time," she proposed.

"I'm all for efficiency."

"Okay. I don't know you, Mr. Foxx, but it seems fairly obvious that you've decided I make a dandy sparring partner."

"Among other things," he said.

"What other things?" she demanded baldly.

He smiled slowly.

When it became obvious that was going to be the

only answer he gave her, Amanda drew a deep breath and released it slowly. "Mind telling me why? I mean, do you have some masochistic need to go after any woman who's pointedly not interested?"

"No." He spoke casually, as if the conversation were about the weather. "There's just something about you, I guess. Your sharp tongue or your red hair. Something."

Amanda stared at him and felt an unexpected flash of amusement. "Chemistry?"

"For want of a better word. Don't you believe in chemistry, Miss Trask?"

"Sure, in a laboratory."

"But not between a man and a woman?"

That little voice in Amanda's head was urging caution; she ignored it, and didn't stop then to wonder why. "Look, I'm not responsible for your, er, chemical reactions."

"In this case," he said calmly, "you certainly are."

"You know what I mean."

"Are you married?"

"No."

"Engaged?"

Amanda shook her head.

"Anybody special?"

"Not at the moment. Mr. Foxx—"

"Let me guess. You've had a tragic past romance and now you're very bitter toward men."

She dropped her gaze to the catalogues in her lap. Damn the man, why wouldn't he stop this? With an effort she held her voice even. "Can't you just accept the fact that I'm not interested?"

"Only if you give me a good reason." He studied

her lowered head, watching the shimmer of firelight on her hair. It occurred to him vaguely that he was pressing too hard, that for some reason this was terribly important to him, but he didn't question that. He'd always listened to his instincts, and right now they were telling him to break through her guard even if he had to use strong tactics to do it.

She looked up at him, and Ryder felt his insides tighten. She was lovely, he thought, and there was something almost fragile about her—not physically, but emotionally. He had the feeling that the chip on her shoulder had been earned, that his light remark about tragic past romances had been closer to the target than he'd expected.

"Mr. Foxx—"

"Ryder." He heard the change in his voice, the note that wasn't mocking or casual but something very serious. And she heard it too; he saw her green eyes widen slightly. "Please," he added quietly.

Amanda tried to keep her guard up, but he was being unfair by suddenly switching tactics like this. It was shockingly difficult to maintain a belligerent front when the man looked at her with an unexpected gentleness in his gray eyes.

"Dammit," she muttered.

Quick amusement curved his firm mouth. "Is it so hard? Just a name, two syllables. And since Miss Nell isn't the only one who knows the meaning behind some names, I'll admit that mine means 'knight' or 'horseman.' "

"Figures," she said, half to herself.

His smile widened. "And yours means 'beloved.' I suppose I could call you that since you won't let me call you Amanda."

"Make it Amanda," she said somewhat hastily, choosing the lesser of two evils.

He lifted an eyebrow and waited.

She eyed him for a moment, then gave in reluctantly. "All right. Make it Amanda . . . Ryder."

"That's a step in the right direction," he noted. "Now for the next one. Do you think we can be friends, Amanda?"

It was her turn to lift an eyebrow. "Friends?"

"Well, for a start. I'm a reasonable man, after all. I don't expect it to be easy."

She shouldn't have said it. She knew that, but Amanda heard the question emerge from her lips. "Don't expect what to be easy?"

"Getting you into my bed."

Amanda blinked. She had heard a number of propositions in her time, but most had been couched in charming euphemisms. Oddly enough, she found his bluntness refreshing. And she didn't know whether to be angry at her own reaction or absolutely appalled.

"That's in the nature of a friendly warning," he explained gravely.

"And I'm supposed to agree to be *friends* with you after hearing it?" she asked dryly.

"Of course. You can always say no when we get to the next step. But—another warning—I don't give up easily."

She shook her head slightly. "I'm not in the market for a fling, thank you very much."

"Did I say anything about a fling?"

"I don't hear you singing 'O Promise me.' "

Ryder chuckled softly. "No. That would be a little premature. We might not hit it off."

"Exactly what I've been trying to tell you," she said with forced patience.

"Yes, but you aren't willing to give us a chance." He leaned toward her slightly, one powerful arm stretched along the back of the couch between them. "Amanda, I'm a businessman. I've learned never to turn away from an opportunity without exploring all the possibilities."

"And I'm an opportunity?"

"I think *we* could be. But we'll never find out unless we explore the possibility."

"Did anybody ever tell you that you have the peculiar effect of water dropping on stone?"

"Constantly." He smiled at her.

That smile, she reflected somewhat helplessly, was lethal. The moonlight hadn't done it justice. She found herself shrugging in what she knew was a ridiculously weak way. "All right, dammit. Friends. But even though you may be on vacation, I'm *working* here, don't forget that."

Having won the battle, Ryder didn't press his advantage. Casually he said, "As a matter of fact, this isn't exactly a vacation for me."

"No?" Amanda relaxed just a bit, but continued to eye him warily.

"No. I was invited here to meet a man to talk about a possible business deal. Cyrus Fortune."

She remembered the name from the guest list. "He's due to arrive on Friday. What kind of business deal? Or is it a state secret?"

"It isn't secret—except in Boston. I wouldn't want my competitors to know about the deal before I have a chance to nail it down. Somebody could try to sneak in and outbid me, and I don't have a lot of capital to play with."

Amanda felt an odd jolt as she realized that *she* could be Ryder's competition. But, no, she thought, that couldn't be. Wilderman Electronics and Foxxfire, Ryder's company, were on different levels of the business; they'd never been competitive. She forced herself to concentrate on what he was saying.

"I'm in the electronics business. So far, it's been mostly toys and games, and heaven knows that's been lucrative. But I want to expand the business, and for that I need an edge."

"An edge?"

"Something to put me well ahead of the competition. There's an independent computer hacker in the Northeast who's been working on a new invention. He's hardly more than a kid, but then, the visionaries in electronics tend to be very young. Anyway, he's come up with a patented new system that's pretty sure to revolutionize the computer industry. I want the rights to that system."

"And he's offering them to you?"

"No, he sold the rights to someone else. Cyrus Fortune. I couldn't find out much about the man, but he seems to be a kind of entrepreneur willing to gamble on a smaller company like mine over some of the bigger ones."

"It sounds like an important deal," Amanda said slowly.

"For my company it's vital," he said. "I don't have the capital to form a research and development team, or the patience to wait years for some kind of breakthrough. Everyone's into games and toys, and there isn't much potential for growth or a bigger slice of the market. Personal computers are the thing now, and the next logical step is a system that runs everything in a house from security to the environment with high efficiency and low cost."

*Dunbar's system.*

She knew about it—all too well. Though she'd never taken much interest in the day-to-day running of the Wilderman business empire, she did keep a close eye on one relatively small part of it.

Wilderman Electronics had been her father's baby. He's started it nearly thirty years before with the design and manufacture of small appliances—radios and the like. When he and his brother formed a partnership and branched out, Patrick Wilderman kept the electronics division separate from the other ventures.

Though Amanda had inherited substantial shares of the family businesses that her uncle Edward now ran, Wilderman Electronics had been left to her alone. It was a public corporation, but since Amanda controlled slightly over sixty percent of the voting stock, her decisions *were* the company's. In addition, Wilderman Electronics was the parent corporation for several smaller divisions, including a nationally known research and development branch.

That particular subsidiary had been trying to get Eric Dunbar on their team for several years.

Dunbar's new system wouldn't make existing technology obsolete—at least not immediately—but it would, as Ryder said, offer a distinct advantage to any company with an eye to the future. And at Wilderman Electronics's most recent board meeting less than two weeks before, a substantial chunk of capital had been earmarked for the sole purpose of acquiring the permanent employment of Eric Dunbar, the rights to his new system, and, if possible, getting the patent itself.

"The wave of the future," she said now, trying to think. "But what if . . . what if you can't get the rights?"

Ryder smiled a bit wryly. "I've been scratching and clawing for ten years to build the company. I wouldn't go under without this new system, but I'd have to go on fighting just to stay afloat. It's a competitive market; I need an edge."

Though she had more than once thought it a curse rather than a blessing, Amanda had taken her personal wealth for granted. It had always been there, and a carefully handpicked group of advisers, accountants, and lawyers virtually assured that it always would be. She had never had to scratch or claw for anything she wanted.

And now she felt like the worst kind of fraud. Heaven knew she hadn't intended to deceive, but here she was, squarely behind the eight ball. Ryder knew her under a false name, and he never would have confided his business plans to her if he'd known who she was. He was fighting for a goal with limited capital; she had access to almost unlimited capital.

For him, it was do or die, with years of struggle ahead of him if he lost the deal. For her, it was a deal that would definitely make a difference—but not that big a difference. Wilderman Electronics had the resources and the time to control a healthy share of the market even without an edge.

He laughed suddenly. "I'm sorry, you can't be interested in all this."

She looked at him and felt trapped. "I—I find it very interesting. I minored in electrical engineering in college."

"What was your major?"

"Business administration."

"So you ended up managing guest ranches?"

Amanda hesitated. "I'm just here to oversee the renovation and decorating."

"And after that? Do you live in Wyoming?"

She felt as if she were skating on very thin ice. "No. As a matter of fact, I live in Boston. The owner of this place lives there; I'd done some work for him in Vermont, and he wanted me for this job."

"You live in Boston? Isn't it odd that we both had to come way out here to meet?"

"Yes," Amanda said. "Very odd."

# *Four*

"It's not the first time that's happened to me," Ryder said consideringly. "I mean, meeting someone from Boston when we were both hundreds or thousands of miles away."

Amanda smiled. "I know, it's happened to me too. I once met a neighbor of mine for the first time in London. And we'd lived near each other for years."

As if the phrase "near each other" had reminded Ryder of the distance between the two of them, he slid closer suddenly and lifted the catalogues from her lap. "Choosing furniture?" he asked, leafing through the topmost brochure quickly.

"Just making a few preliminary decisions," she replied, trying not to think of how close he was. But he *was* close, and all her senses were reacting to him. She was so involved in trying to ignore her senses that she was just a fraction too late in reacting when he leaned forward to drop the catalogues onto the coffee table and then returned to her side.

It all happened very quickly, she realized somewhat dazedly. Without a wasted motion Ryder had lifted her legs across his lap, keeping one arm over her thighs and slipping the other around her shoulders. She was half lying in the corner of the couch, conscious of his hard thighs beneath hers and his powerful arms holding her prisoner.

Trapped, she felt unnervingly helpless.

Her hands had lifted instinctively to his chest, braced to hold him off. But Ryder made no attempt to use force. Instead, he smiled down at her, a curiously apologetic smile that still managed to hold a great deal of masculine triumph.

"I couldn't stand it anymore," he explained softly.

Since she didn't have to hold him off, Amanda realized that her fingers were moving just a little of their own volition, probing through his thick sweater to find the hard flesh beneath. She tried to make them stop, but the silent command couldn't seem to reach that far.

"You're—moving too fast," she managed to protest in a strained voice.

"Am I?" He shook his head slightly. "I don't think so. I've got the feeling if I give you too much time to think, you'll run away from me."

"That's ridiculous. I'm a grown woman. I don't—I don't run away from men."

"I'm glad to hear it." His voice was deepening, growing a little rough. "Do you know there are secrets in your eyes?"

"What?" She was startled, uneasy.

The arm around her shoulders shifted so that his fingers tangled in her thick hair, holding her head firmly. "No, don't look away. Amanda?"

Warily she met his gaze again, wondering what on earth was happening to her strength of will. He seemed to have the knack of eroding it.

"Amazing eyes," he murmured, his own probing almost unconsciously. "So green. Even now, in an almost dark room, they're green. It isn't fair for you to have eyes so green."

The long fingers moving in her hair were unexpectedly pleasurable; she could literally feel her ability to think clearly slipping away, dissipating like smoke in the wind. All the things she knew she should tell him were locked inside her somewhere, and she couldn't find them, couldn't shape the words. She could only look at him and wonder on some distant level of herself what was happening to her.

"Damn those eyes," he said on a long breath, then lowered his head until his mouth touched hers.

Amanda felt a hot shiver of pure need ripple through her body at the first touch of his lips. Her mouth opened to him instantly, and she felt as well as heard the strange, muted sound in the back of her throat.

He kissed her with utter absorption, as if there were nothing in the world except the two of them and this urgent desire rising inexorably between them. His mouth was hard, yet it seduced rather than demanded, beguiled rather than forced.

She was half conscious of her arms sliding up around his neck, of her fingers twining in the thick silk of his dark hair. Never in her life had she felt anything like the need inside her; it was shattering in its intensity, and she could no more fight it than she could stop breathing. When his lips finally left hers she murmured a husky protest, not even aware of doing so.

"Amanda," he said tautly as his mouth moved slowly down over the warm flesh of her throat.

Hearing her name from him surprised her somehow, and she understood dimly that it was because her identity was overwhelmed by this passion between them. She could recall reading novels where the women had "lost themselves" in passion, and because she herself had never caught fire, she'd been able to sneer inwardly at those weaklings. But now she understood—and it frightened her.

He made her surrender to feelings she couldn't control. The need he aroused in her swamped her willpower, shattered reason until she was defenseless with want.

The realization was a shock, and if it wasn't strong enough to fully penetrate the hot veils of passion, at least it allowed her a shaken protest.

"Ryder . . . it's too fast . . . please . . ."

He lifted his head slowly, gazing down at her with hot eyes. His face was hard, the features masklike with intensity. "I want you," he said softly, roughly.

Amanda could feel her entire throbbing body weaken. She fought desperately for control. "It's too soon," she whispered. "We hardly know each other. Ryder—"

"Do you think that matters?" His voice was raspy. "I knew when you fell off that damned ladder and I caught you."

"*I* didn't know," she protested. "I still don't. I won't just tumble into bed with a stranger, dammit!"

Ryder lowered his head and captured her mouth again. And this time there was force, intensity; this time there was a stark assurance. He took her mouth as if there were no question it belonged to him, that *she* belonged to him.

Amanda heard that strange sound escape again, that muted sound of unthinking pleasure. She felt as if she were sinking down into something hot and dark, being pulled irresistibly by some power beyond her understanding.

He raised his head slowly, staring down at her. She looked as shaken as he felt, as bewildered. Her lovely face was a little pale, her beautiful green eyes dazed and enormous, her lips swollen and reddened from his kisses. He wanted to lift her in his arms and carry her upstairs, to find a room with a bed and lock the door and shut out the world.

He had never felt desire like this, not so all-consuming. He was conscious of a stunning, gut-wrenching need to bury himself in her, to take her so utterly and completely that even the secrets in her eyes would be his.

His own stark need shook him, and because he was a man who had marked out the paths of his life with unerring certainty, this unexpected detour made him abruptly wary. He saw the same uneasy guardedness stirring in her eyes, and even though some part of him hated that look, another part understood.

"All right," he said, surprised by the hoarse sound of his own voice. "I'll try to slow down."

He drew away from her, allowing her to sit up

again beside him. The voice of caution in his head told him to back off emotionally as well as physically, but he couldn't help adding, "Don't make me wait too long."

A spark of green fire showed in her eyes, and she sent him a look that was an odd mixture of defiance and vulnerability. "Don't be so sure of yourself!" she snapped with only the slightest tremor in her voice.

Ryder stood up and pulled her to her feet, then lifted one hand to turn her face up firmly. "Shouldn't I be?" he asked her very softly.

"Damn you," she whispered, her gaze falling before the certainty in his eyes. "You're a *stranger*—"

"No, I'm not. You know me, Amanda. And I know you. It doesn't matter that we met hours ago."

"Lust at first sight," she said jerkily with an attempt at scorn.

"Call it anything you like. It's real, we both know that. I want you. And you want me."

She bit her bottom lip. "I'm old enough to know that what I may want isn't always good for me."

He bent his head and kissed her, keeping it light even though the strain of holding back seemed as if it might tear him in half. "I'll be good for you," he promised.

Amanda didn't reply to that. There didn't seem to be anything she could say.

He didn't seem to expect anything. "I'll walk you to your room," he said.

She watched him bend to pick up the catalogues, then walked beside him silently as they went upstairs. Nemo went with them, his presence as unobtrusive as it could be for a dog of his size.

Ryder left her at her door with a casual good night.

Amanda was more confused than ever. She piled the catalogues on her nightstand and sat down on the bed, looking around the room with eyes that didn't really see it.

"What do I do now, dog?" she murmured to Nemo.

From his position on a faded rug near the foot of her bed, the big dog thumped his tail against the floor and gazed at her with his mild, startled eyes.

"That's a lot of help," she told him.

She was an honest woman by nature, and her impulse was to tell Ryder who she was. She had meant to do just that once she'd discovered why he was here. But somehow the words got lost before she could say them.

This situation was different from any she'd had to deal with. For the first time in her adult life she was reasonably sure that a man was interested in her for herself, that he was attracted to her and wanted her because her eyes were green or her hair was red, or because of the way she looked in jeans. That he was drawn to her because of one or more of the many mysterious reasons that drew a man to a woman.

It wasn't her name or family, or the healthy status of her bank account.

Yet that same man was here for the purpose of building his company up to compete with hers.

She didn't know what to do. Tell him the truth? Explain that her being here was just a coincidence? She doubted he'd believe her. She didn't believe it herself.

Amanda rose and went to her dresser, opening the top drawer and gazing down at what she had discovered in her suitcase when she'd finished unpacking last night.

The glass shoe.

Samantha must have put it there, Amanda had realized. Another one of her gentle reminders. But she couldn't—*surely she couldn't*—have had anything to do with sending Ryder here? No, that was just ridiculous. Ryder had come here to meet with a man about a business matter.

Amanda wanted to forget about the Cinderella masquerade, particularly since Ryder had clearly forgotten all about it. But she couldn't. That had been the first deceit, no matter how innocent; not telling Ryder who she was now was the second deceit.

She thought he might well forgive the first because it had been innocent. But what would he think if she told him now that she was a Wilderman and controlled Wilderman Electronics?

"Why can't it be as simple as a fairy tale?" she murmured aloud.

It wasn't until she was in bed sometime later that Amanda realized something. Hostility hadn't worked. Guardedness hadn't worked. But if she told Ryder who she really was, she had little doubt that his interest in her as a woman would vanish like smoke.

How ironic. The first man interested in her for herself alone could well be the first man to be more angry than impressed by who she was.

The realization should have comforted her. After all, revealing her true identity would resolve the dilemma. She wouldn't have to be wary of being hurt again. She wouldn't have to guard her tongue or examine every word before she spoke. She could be herself again.

It was a long time before she fell asleep.


"Amanda, Jeff Haynes just called me."

She kept her gaze fixed on the landing above, wary of having someone—especially a particular someone—overhear her conversation with her uncle. Since he was an early riser, she hadn't hesitated to call him at virtually the crack of dawn. "And he told you that a man named Cyrus Fortune had bought the rights to Dunbar's patent?"

There was a long silence, and then Edward Wilderman said somewhat dryly, "So you've heard."

"Yes. What did Jeff say about it?" Jeffrey Haynes was the CEO of Wilderman Electronics, and a good friend of Edward's. He was also Amanda's godfather.

"Well, Dunbar's on the verge of signing an employment agreement, but he says the patent's out of reach."

Amanda hesitated, then slowly asked, "Uncle Edward, did you know that Ryder Foxx would be here?"

After a hesitation of his own, her uncle said, "Samantha was planning something, but I gather it fell through; she swears it isn't her doing. He's there to meet with Cyrus Fortune?"

"Yes."

Edward sighed. "When I heard Fortune's name, I remembered he was one of the guests. But Amanda, Ryder Foxx's name wasn't on the list. Cyrus Fortune made reservations for himself—and a guest, unnamed. He was asked to notify the ranch directly, to give Penny the guest's name and both arrival times."

Amanda drew a breath. "Could Fortune have planned so far in advance? The reservations were made months ago. How could he have been so sure of getting the patent from Dunbar?"

"He couldn't have been," Edward said immediately. "The system wasn't even ready then. It has to be a fluke, Amanda. When Fortune made the reservations, we didn't own the ranch. He got the rights to the patent, then invited Ryder Foxx to be his guest and talk about it."

"All right, so it's a fluke. But what now? I can't make Fortune an offer for the patent, Uncle Edward. I just can't."

"Why not? You're empowered—"

"That isn't it. Look, Cyrus Fortune knows you own the ranch because your office communicated with him about the renovations. Right?"

"Right."

"But Ryder Foxx *doesn't* know. The ranch is officially owned by a subsidiary based in Texas, the same one that owns the ranch down there. The Wilderman name isn't even connected to this place. I mean, granted, Ryder could have found out easily enough, but why would he? He believes he's just here to meet a man and talk about a business deal."

"So?" Edward asked.

"So Cyrus Fortune had to know that you'd know where he was as soon as the news broke about the patent. And since you own this place, he wouldn't doubt that you—or I—would send someone out here to make him an offer. It may have started out as a fluke, but what if Fortune's planning to take advantage of the situation?"

"You mean play you and Ryder Foxx against each other?"

"Why not? Maybe he's interested in a little healthy competition. And how do you suppose Ryder will feel when he discovers he's on Wilderman property with the owner of Wilderman Electronics here as well?"

"Outgunned," Edward said dryly.

"And I'm using Mother's name," Amanda said. "It looks so damned deceitful."

"It's just a series of flukes, Amanda. That we bought the ranch, that I sent you out there, and that you tend to use your mother's name."

"In Ryder's place, would you believe that?"

After a moment he said, "Probably not."

"Neither would I."

"Look, honey, the man understands competition. I realize the patent could mean expansion for him, but—"

"It would mean the same thing for us. But Uncle Edward, it's Ryder's chance to establish his company as an important presence in the electronics industry."

"Amanda, are you seriously saying that you plan to stand by without lifting a finger and watch Ryder Foxx acquire the rights to a system that would put his company at least five years ahead of your own?"

Softly she said, "Wilderman could play catch-up for five years with no major damage. I don't think Foxxfire could."

His own voice softened, Edward said, "That's not a very businesslike decision, honey."

"I know."

"Are you going to tell him who you are?"

She laughed a bit shakily. "What choice do I have? Ten to one Cyrus Fortune will know, and I can't see him keeping a piece of information like that to himself. He's supposed to arrive on Friday, so I have today and tomorrow. I'd rather that Ryder find out from me. But I just don't know how to tell him."

"I get the feeling that Sam's matchmaking struck a few sparks this time. Am I right?"

"It doesn't matter."

"Maybe it does matter. Amanda, I've met Ryder Foxx. He's ambitious, even ruthless to a certain extent. But he's honest, and he fights fair. He's had chances to marry money if he wanted take the easy way. But he didn't. I don't believe he ever would. And I'll tell you something else I don't believe he'll do."

"What?"

"I don't believe he'll take the easy way this time. Once he knows who you are, I think he'll expect you to go after those rights just as hard as he."

Amanda put a great deal of faith in her uncle's judgments about people; he was seldom off on his perceptions and intuitions. And her own instincts had been telling her the same things about Ryder. Still, she had to protest. "But he told me he wanted to nail the deal down before the competition could . . . could sneak in and outbid him."

"Logical. But the competition's *there*, honey. He's used to fighting for what he wants. He isn't the kind of man who likes winning for its own sake."

"Damn," she murmured.

"I just wanted to warn you."

"All right. Thanks, Uncle Edward. I'll get through it somehow."

"Good luck."

Amanda cradled the phone, staring at it without seeing it. How on earth was she going to "get through" this situation and emerge intact?

"Amanda?"

She forced the jumbled thoughts into the back of her mind. "Morning, Penny."

"Morning. Doug just came up from the corral to say your horse was ready. But so is breakfast. Aren't you hungry? You missed supper last night."

Amanda shrugged. "I don't have much of an appetite. Penny . . . could you do me a favor?"

"Sure. Name it."

"You're the only one here besides me who knows that Edward Wilderman owns this place; could you keep it to yourself for a while? There's a business deal in the offing."

The housekeeper nodded incuriously. "Okay. Nemo's in the kitchen eating his breakfast, so you'd better slip out while he's distracted. It looks like he's adopted you, and he doesn't get along too well with the horses. Look, don't ride out too far or be gone too long. I just heard a weather bulletin and there's a storm coming in."

That, Amanda reflected, was all she needed. "I'll be out only an hour or so."

"I'll keep your breakfast warm."

"You don't have to—"

Penny cut her off with a dismissing gesture. "It's no trouble. Besides, if you start living on your nerves, we'll all be in trouble. From the looks of things, you're going to need your strength."

Amanda was left to ponder that as Penny disappeared back down the hallway to the kitchen. She wasn't sure if the housekeeper had meant the problems of guests in a house under renovation, or if she had noticed other problems.

The sound of a door closing upstairs sent Amanda quickly out of the house. It was quite definitely cold outside, the sun just rising on a clouded horizon, and she zipped up her quilted jacket and pulled on warm gloves as she made her way down to the corral.

"Morning, Amanda," Doug called, emerging from the stock barn as she approached. He met her and, after a glance around to make certain they wouldn't be overheard by the few men who were doing the early morning feeding and watering of the stock, said, "Edward told me you might be working on this place, so I brought Whiskey up from Texas."

"Oh, thanks, Doug." She felt instantly more cheerful, and smiled at the middle-aged foreman.

Doug Chandler oversaw all the Wilderman ranching concerns, handpicking men and stock, then remaining at each place until it was established and he could safely leave someone else in charge. He knew Amanda well, since she spent several weeks each year on the Texas ranch.

He nodded toward the big, heavily muscled quarter horse tied to the corral's top rail. "He's ready for you. But watch him. He's still sulking. I hauled him up with some other stock, and you know how he hates road travel."

Amanda laughed. "Yes, I know. I shouldn't be out more than an hour or so."

"Okay." He waved and headed back for the barn.

She went over to the big sorrel, careful to approach his head. Whiskey was a definite handful with a low tolerance for people—and just about everything else. As a young stallion he'd been wildly savage, and though gelding had left him relatively manageable, he still retained his uncertain temper and his stubborn resistance to authority. He was ten years old now, and Doug had often sworn that if he hadn't been the best cowhorse in Texas, somebody would have taken a shotgun to him years ago.

Amanda liked the horse because he kept her on her toes. He was apt to kick or bite, and had a number of other bad habits calculated to unnerve a rider. But he tolerated her more than most people, so the bite he aimed at her now was more or less automatic and halfhearted, and she avoided it easily.

"Be nice," she warned him, untying the reins and checking the girth. Out of the corner of her eye she saw Whiskey send her a glance, his ears back. He'd held his breath while Doug had tightened the girth, so now it was too loose to hold the saddle securely. Amanda tightened it firmly and quickly, checked the length of the stirrups, and then mounted the horse before he could think of trying something else.

She felt his back bow up in a prelude to bucking as she turned him away from the fence, but he settled down after a few steps, obviously deciding not to bother trying to throw her; he'd been trying that for more than five years, and had yet to succeed. He moved out in his easy, ground-covering trot, obeying Amanda's guiding touch on the reins to head northwest toward the Bighorn Mountains.

Amanda had no particular destination in mind. She just wanted to give the cold air a chance to blow away a few cobwebs in her mind. She opened and closed several gates without dismounting, riding steadily northwest and enjoying the chill wind on her face. They passed through several stands of cattle, and Whiskey flicked an ear back at her, but since he obviously wasn't expected to work today, he made no attempt to herd the cattle and get them moving.

She stopped finally, almost an hour later, near a couple of cottonwood trees, and it wasn't until then that she realized she wasn't going to be alone. Between the wind in her face and the rhythmic creaking of the saddle, she had heard nothing, but as soon as she and the horse were still she heard approaching hoofbeats.

She turned Whiskey to see who it was, and felt little surprise when she saw Ryder coming toward her. He was on a big gray gelding, and by the way he sat easily in the saddle Amanda knew that he'd been riding for years.

"Don't you know it's freezing out here?" he called.

"Don't you?" she retorted.

Ryder pulled up abreast of her so that their horses were standing side by side but facing in opposite directions. He was wearing a thickly quilted jacket, jeans, gloves, and boots as she was. And, just as she, he was hatless.

"I'm hot-natured," he said. "Cold weather doesn't bother me at all."

Amanda eyed him. "I don't think I want to touch that remark," she said.

"Not up to my weight this morning?"

Totally against her will she felt a sensual heat as she thought of his weight on her. Hoping her cheeks were already reddened by the cold, she managed to say lightly, "I'm not a morning person. Sue me."

He studied her thoughtfully, his eyes bright. "You're being elusive," he said in a considering tone. "Last night scared you, didn't it?"

Her first impulse was to deny that unequivocally, but a saner voice prevailed. What was the use of denying what was obvious, she thought wryly. She touched her heels to Whiskey's sides so that he started walking back toward the ranch house, and waited until Ryder brought his own horse alongside before she spoke.

"I suppose it'll pander to your ego if I say yes," she muttered.

"No." He was silent for a moment. "The opposite, I think. I don't want to scare you, Amanda. Fear doesn't belong between a man and a woman."

She kept her gaze focused ahead, a little surprised by what he said but unwilling to show it. She tried to nerve herself up to tell him who she was but, again, couldn't find the words to explain.

"You've been hurt, haven't you?" he said suddenly.

This time it required a supreme effort not to turn her head and look at him. "Haven't we all?" she said flippantly.

A large, gloved hand reached over to cover hers

and draw back on the reins. She felt Ryder's knee brush hers, and was dimly surprised that Whiskey didn't sidle or kick in his usual objection to being crowded by another horse. Maybe he was mellowing, she thought.

"Amanda, look at me."

He'd bewitched her horse. He'd bewitched her. She turned her head and looked at him. He was too close, and the intensity of him enveloped her.

"What are you afraid of? Being hurt again? I don't want to hurt you."

She heard the ghost of a laugh escape her. "Do you think that matters?"

A slight frown drew his brows together. "Don't good intentions count?"

"You know what they say about the road to hell." She pushed his hand away from the reins. Now was the moment, she thought. Now she had to tell him the truth. But she was feeling too much to shape the truth into words. She was feeling so much that she didn't know *what* she felt.

Ryder was staring at her, his sharp gray eyes narrowed. But before he could say anything, Amanda realized that it was beginning to snow.

"We'd better get back," she said. "There's a storm coming." She lifted the reins slightly and her horse obediently moved forward.

The man riding beside her said nothing for several minutes. Then, quietly, he said, "He must have hurt you very badly."

Surprising herself, Amanda replied to that honestly. "Hearts don't break, Ryder. *We* don't break. We just make stupid mistakes."

"What mistake did you make?"

She thought about that, then managed a smile even though she wasn't looking at him. "I think I made the mistake of expectations. It isn't a particularly original story." She was mocking herself now, trying to keep it light. "I expected him to be honest. He wasn't."

"And you got hurt."

Her own words had caused guilt to sweep over her, and Amanda chided herself angrily. Dammit, *why* couldn't she tell him the truth? She responded to his comment almost absently. "I also got over it."

"Did you?"

She decided not to answer that. Instead, she said, "We'd better hurry," and urged Whiskey into a lope before Ryder could accuse her of running away.

The remainder of the ride back to the ranch was accomplished in silence. By the time they drew up near the house, the light snow had become big, wet flakes blown by a stiff wind, and visibility was decreasing rapidly.

"I'll take them to the barn," Ryder said. "You go on into the house."

Amanda dismounted and handed him her reins. "Thanks. Doug will unsaddle them."

"See you inside."

She went into the house, shaking the snow off her jacket and hair as she stood just inside the kitchen door on a braided rug. She tucked her gloves into the pockets of her jacket, then hung it up on a peg by the door. She took one step into the warmth of the big kitchen, but was halted by the large, unhappy dog standing squarely before her. He gave her a look of heart-rending reproach.

"I'm sorry," she said involuntarily. "But we went a long way, and you would have gotten tired."

Nemo waved his tail in acknowledgment but whined low in his throat, still unhappy.

Amanda looked across the room at Penny, who was busy mixing the ingredients for a cake. "What's wrong with him?" she asked Penny.

"He doesn't like storms," Penny said calmly. "The last time I saw him this upset, we were snowed in for a week."

Amanda winced. "Great. It's really coming down out there."

"I know. The work crew turned around and left no sooner than they got here. The foreman said to tell you they'd be back when the weather cleared. Nobody wanted to get stuck this far from town. Your breakfast is in the top oven."

"I really don't—"

"Eat," Penny insisted without looking at her.

It was less trouble to give in. Amanda patted Nemo on his massive head, then crossed the room and poured herself a cup of coffee. "Where's Sharon?"

"I sent her to town with one of the men. Supplies, just in case."

"I hope they make it back all right," Amanda said uneasily.

"Don't worry. They went in that new four-wheel-drive Doug brought with him."

Amanda set her coffee cup on the old wooden table pushed over in one corner, deciding to eat in the kitchen rather than in lonely splendor in the dining room. She went to the two ovens that were built-in and opened the top one. Two plates were inside, both heaped with pancakes and crisp bacon.

"Ryder?" Amanda asked, sending Penny a questioning look.

"Uh-huh," Penny murmured, industriously mixing batter. "He asked where you were. As soon as I told him, he headed for the barn."

"Oh," Amanda said.

The back door opened suddenly, admitting a gust of cold air and a snow-covered Ryder. "Did somebody say something about a storm?" he demanded as he forced the door shut behind him. "That's no storm out there. That's a blizzard."

# *Five*

---

Without replying to his announcement, Amanda retrieved both plates from the oven and carried them to the table. "Coffee's over there," she said with a nod when he'd removed his gloves and jacket. She found napkins and silverware for them both, and carried them to the table, then sat down and began eating her breakfast.

Ryder joined her with his coffee, whistling under his breath, seemingly cheerful for a man who anticipated being snowed in for days to come.

Amanda tried to keep her mind off that probability. "Penny, what about the other guests?"

Penny shrugged philosophically. "We're ready for them, but I'm not going to hold my breath. The next was due to arrive tomorrow; another few hours and the roads are going to be impassable. I'd say until this blows over, it's going to be just us."

Just the four of them, Amanda reflected. Just her,

Penny, Sharon, and Ryder. There were more than a dozen ranch hands out in the bunkhouse, of course, but that was self-contained; the men had their own kitchen, their own cook, and their own work to do—even in a blizzard.

Amanda felt a little desperate. With only the four of them in the house, there was barely enough work for Penny and Sharon, let alone her. She could do virtually none of the work she'd come to the ranch to do, since the workmen wouldn't be around. Quite literally, there was nothing for her to manage. Except far too much free time.

And a guest who wanted her.

She stole a glance at the man sitting across from her, and found him regarding her with a faint smile.

"Don't look so worried," he said softly for her ears alone.

Amanda knew at that moment, with utter clarity, that she had to tell him the truth about herself. Now, before this—whatever it was—between them went any further. She looked down at her half-empty plate, then rose and carried it to the sink.

"I'll take care of that," Penny said, taking the plate away from her.

Nodding, Amanda went silently out of the kitchen. She went down the hall and into the den, knowing Ryder would follow her. Having made her decision at last, she felt an odd kind of peace. No, she realized, not peace. A sense of suspension. A waiting.

"Amanda?"

There was a fire in the fireplace, blazing merrily. Penny must have built it, Amanda thought as she stood before the smoke-blackened old brick hearth and turned to face him. "There's something I have to tell you."

He crossed the room slowly until he reached the couch. "Should I sit down?" he asked politely.

She nodded. "Yes."

He did, his expression growing a bit more serious as her tension obviously communicated itself to him. "Okay. I'm braced for it."

Amanda tried to think of the best way to explain this. She'd known it would be difficult, but . . . "Have you ever worked for a relative?"

"No. I don't have many."

"Well, it's easier sometimes if the people around you don't know that you're related to the boss."

Ryder nodded. "I can see how it would be. And so?"

She drew a breath and looked away from him, watching Nemo enter the room and lie down on a rug near the door. "And so, since I often work for my uncle, I prefer to do so as just another employee. And because we have the same last name, I use my mother's maiden name whenever I'm doing a job for him." She looked back at Ryder.

"Your name isn't Trask?" He seemed very still, his eyes narrowing as he gazed at her.

"No." She rushed on before he could asked the next logical question. "When I came out here I didn't know who was on the guest list. It wasn't until you told me why you'd come that I realized things were going to be . . . tangled." Of all the incoherent explanations, she thought a bit wildly, this had to be the worst.

"Who are you?" Ryder asked, his voice suddenly flat.

She folded her arms beneath her breasts, wondering why, between them, the furnace and the fire weren't heating the room. She felt cold. "I'm—Amanda Wilderman."

After a moment he said, "Wilderman Electronics." It wasn't a question.

But she answered. "Yes."

"You own the company."

She nodded. "I don't have much to do with the day-to-day running of it. But I knew about Dunbar's patent, knew we were trying to get the rights. Until you told me, I hadn't known that they'd been sold at all, much less to a guest about to arrive here."

"Do you expect me to believe that?"

Amanda could find nothing in his voice or his face. No emotion at all. He was just watching her, his eyes shuttered. She shook her head slightly and heard a touch of bitterness in her own voice. "I learned a lot about expectations, remember? No, I don't expect you to believe me."

"Is it the truth?"

"Yes. I didn't know you'd be here. I didn't know that Cyrus Fortune had bought the rights to Dunbar's system, or anything else about him. He was just a name on a list of guests." She felt tired.

Ryder got up from the couch and moved until he was standing an arm's length from her. "I believe you," he said.

Amanda stared up at him. "What?"

"I said I believe you."

She was startled. "Why?" she asked slowly.

"Several reasons." He was looking down at her, his eyes grave. "I don't think you'd lie about it, for one thing. You aren't the type for that. But the most convincing reason is purely practical."

"And that is?"

"The fact that you wouldn't have anything to gain by such an elaborate deception, as far as I can see. I mean, why the cloak and dagger? You don't have to resort to such tricks. Unless I'm much mistaken about your company, you have the resources to offer a hell of a lot more than I could possibly come up with."

"So why . . . why muddy the water?"

"Exactly. You have no reason to do that. Are you going after the rights, by the way?"

Amanda temporized, very reluctant to make this an issue between them. "We were, naturally. Maybe we don't need that new system of his."

Ryder studied her for a moment, his eyes slightly narrowed. "I think we're going to have to talk about that," he said slowly. Then he shrugged, clearly pushing the matter aside for the moment.

She knew what he was thinking about because she could read the intent behind darkening gray eyes. Physically she responded instantly, a slow heat uncurling inside her, a tremor shaking her muscles. Emotionally she felt a little numb, having expected him to withdraw from her in anger, having been braced for that.

It was unnerving.

He took a half step closer, still not touching her.

"Is that what you've been worried about? Because you thought I'd be mad when I found out who you were?"

"It crossed my mind," she said as steadily as she could.

"Did you want me to be mad?" he asked perceptively. "To back off, maybe?"

Amanda hesitated. "That crossed my mind too," she confessed finally.

"You don't have to look for excuses to push me away. All you have to do is tell me to get lost, Amanda." His hands rose, finding her hips and drawing her slowly toward him. "Just tell me you don't want me."

She saw her hands reach up with a mind of their own to rest on his chest, pale against the black of his sweatshirt, the long fingers nervous and without assurance. The insistent guidance of his hands brought her closer until she felt the hard strength of his body against her. Even through the denim of their jeans she could feel the heat of him, and when he moved subtly her breath caught in her throat.

"Just tell me," he repeated softly, his voice a little husky now.

That was a fine thing to point out to her, she thought somewhat wildly. Just tell him? When he was touching her like this so that she could barely think? She forced herself to string words together, to be coherent. "You said—you'd slow down."

He smiled, the curve of his firm lips somehow peculiarly devilish. "Haven't you noticed? I'm taking pains to move with extreme slowness."

Something escaped Amanda's lips, and she wasn't sure if it was a smothered laugh or a choked sound of despair. It could have been either. On the edge of her consciousness she was aware of the wind wailing softly outside, and she thought of snowbound days ahead, and of Ryder moving slowly—like a stalking cat.

"There isn't going to be much for either of us to do during this storm," he said, obviously thinking along the same lines. "Except get to know each other."

Looking up into his darkened gray eyes, Amanda felt a wave of panic unlike anything she'd ever known before. It was raw, almost primal, as if it came from someplace inside her too deep for words. She half closed her eyes, the shock of that feeling jolting through her and leaving behind it a kind of numb bewilderment.

"Amanda?"

She felt one of his hands lift to her neck, his thumb pushing her chin up gently. "I don't—" she began, having no idea what she was going to say.

"I do," he muttered, as if he knew. His head bent, his dark eyes fixed on her mouth.

She couldn't turn away, couldn't escape him. And when his warm, hard lips covered hers, the surge of pleasure was so intense that her knees almost buckled. The hand at her hip slipped lower, shaping rounded flesh, and held her firmly against him. His other hand slid around to the nape of her neck, under her hair, the fingers moving caressingly against her scalp.

Amanda could feel her hands move up, over the thick material of his sweatshirt. Her eyes were closed, yet she saw through her touching fingers. The shirt, rough and dark. The base of his neck, hard and warm, a pulse beating under his flesh with a quickening rhythm, a tiny heartbeat caged. Then his hair, thick and soft, like silk.

He was kissing her with that strangely moving absorption that made her feel singular, unique. All his attention was fixed on her, on this slow exploring. There was nothing tentative about him, yet she had the odd feeling that he was somehow . . . gauging her response. When he finally lifted his head and looked down at her, she was sure of it. There was something like triumph in his eyes, and the curve of his mouth was stamped with an unmistakable masculine arrogance.

"I definitely do," he said.

She wanted to wipe that look off his face, conscious of a bitter resentment that he could do this to her. How could he and be so detached from it himself? She was shaking, her legs weak; she was filled with a heated dizziness that sapped strength. Her whole body ached with a yearning she'd never felt before. She tried to make her arms stop clinging to the strong column of his neck, but they wouldn't move. It made her furious.

"Cage your ego, will you?" she managed to say in a voice that was supposed to be biting but quavered instead.

He looked surprised. "It isn't ego." The hand at her nape moved slowly down her back until it joined the other one to curve over her bottom. "I'm glad you want me as much as I want you, that's all."

*It isn't just that. It's*—Amanda didn't have to complete the thought in her mind. She knew what that final word was. Final—dear Lord.

That was why she responded to him like this, why she lost herself in this raw, compelling desire for him. That was why she had felt sheer panic sweep over her with such stunning force.

Because she was falling in love with him.

The panic was still there, hovering on the edge of her consciousness, but Amanda knew that was only a woman's instinctive fear of her own vulnerability. There was, after all, no other reason for fear. Whatever his own feelings for her, Ryder's desire had been obvious long before he'd found out who she was. It was she he wanted. Not her company. Not her bank account.

"What are you thinking?" he asked, his voice roughening a bit.

Amanda realized that she'd gone totally still as realization flooded through her. She looked up at him, aware suddenly that he wasn't as much in control as she'd thought he was. And he definitely was not detached. There was a tightness around his jaw that spoke of something tautly reined, and the hands holding her against him were restless, kneading slowly. Even through the thick material of their jeans she was burningly conscious of the hard ridge of desire pressed so intimately to her yielding softness.

"I'm . . . not thinking of anything," she said finally, her voice low.

Ryder gazed into her wide green eyes, wanting just to yank her up into his arms and find a bed. There was something aloof in her, and it was driving him crazy. She couldn't be reserved with him once she was his, he was sure of that. Reasonably sure, anyway. With Amanda it was difficult to be sure of anything. She baffled him, and he wasn't accustomed to being puzzled by a woman.

She possessed the damnedest control he'd ever run into. As prickly as brambles, she was wary, guarded, allowing very little of herself to escape. He knew she'd been hurt, and the way she sometimes looked at him with a kind of defensive uncertainty made him long to get his hands on whoever had done that to her.

Given her background, he would have expected her to be—what? More casual about a possible affair? No, not that exactly. But . . . well, less surprised, perhaps? Yes, he thought, that was it. She was surprised by him, by this desire between them. Surprised by her own response.

Well, hell, he was surprised about himself. He'd certainly enjoyed several relationships during the past, but most of his attention—single-minded, he knew—had been fixed on building his company. But now, with Amanda, he was aware that the center of himself had shifted somehow, his focus changed. He felt oddly intent, hungry in a way he'd never felt before. And the feeling was intensifying.

She felt it too; that was what he'd discovered. She felt this overpowering desire. Her response to him was instant, passionate. In his arms the barriers dissolved, and she took fire.

Fire . . .

"Ryder?" She was a little uneasy, wariness creeping into her heartbreaking eyes.

Something nagged at him, some vague thing on the tip of his mind, but he ignored it. He bent his head and kissed her, holding his own desire rigidly in check despite the screaming insistence of every nerve in his body. The faint stiffness he'd felt in her melted away as she responded, and he heard that kittenlike sound she had made before. Damn, it went through him like an electrical current, that little sound in the back of her throat, that little soft purr of pleasure.

Kissing her was more exciting than sex had been with other women, and the promise of what was to come had him on the ragged edge of control. He wasn't a patient man by nature, but he had learned to be patient if the goal was worth it. This goal, he thought, was quite definitely worth it.

But when he raised his head and looked down at her, he felt his control slip yet another notch. Her eyes were sleepy with passion, her face was a little flushed, beautifully rosy. And her mouth . . . lips parted, moist, slightly swollen from his kisses.

"I don't know how much longer I can wait." He heard the words escape him, heard the guttural sounds of them, and knew it was the stark truth.

For an instant, just a fleeting second, he thought she was going to give in to the desire between them. But then uncertainty and doubt clouded her eyes. He wondered what she was thinking.

Expectations. That was what she'd said. That she'd expected a man to be honest with her and he hadn't been. Was that bothering her now? Did she think this involvement was casual for him? Was that it?

An appetite to be satisfied and she just happened to be handy? "Amanda—"

She pulled her arms from around his neck and pushed against his chest. Reluctantly he released her. Dammit, he felt like an adolescent, consumed with the urge to grab her. He reminded himself fiercely that he wasn't a teenager, that he could control himself. It only half worked, but half was good enough.

Turning toward the fire and staring down at it, she said in a low, hurried voice, "I don't mean to be a . . . a tease. But I don't know you very well, and—"

"And nice girls don't sleep with strangers?" He was getting control of his voice, at least. It didn't sound quite so intense as before.

"I guess. We're raised that way." A faint smile touched her lips.

"Just tell me you want me," he said, a little surprised by his need to hear her admit it. But it was a need he couldn't control, couldn't mute; his need was something that had to be satisfied.

She half shrugged, a helpless movement, and sent him a flickering glance. "I haven't been able to hide that very well. You—you have to know it."

"Tell me, Amanda." He reached out and gently turned her face toward him, his fingers lingering almost compulsively to stroke the warm flesh of her throat.

She stared up at him, unnerved by his intensity. He knew it, of course he did. He could *see* it. Her legs were still weak, and she was trembling. But he wanted her to say it, and she couldn't fight the demand in his eyes.

"I want you," she said unsteadily, her voice hardly more than a whisper.

He stroked her cheek once, lightly, with just the tips of his fingers, and then his hand fell to his side. He was surprised at the effort it took to stop touching her. "I don't want us to be strangers in bed, Amanda," he said quietly.

He was willing to give her time, she realized. How much time she didn't know. If the storm outside fulfilled its promise, they could be snowbound for days. Virtually alone, cut off from the world. The solitude would provide an intimacy with few barriers between them. But there were precious few barriers anyway. She knew that if he had gone on kissing her, holding her, if he had said, "Now," she wouldn't have been able to protest.

She nodded slowly. "Then, maybe I should go and dig out that desk of cards."

It wasn't at all easy to be less self-conscious around a man who assumed—with some justification—that you'd be sharing his bed eventually, but Amanda was gradually able to relax. It helped that Ryder had backed off somewhat, his intensity gone or hidden now, and that he possessed an easy charm and a sense of humor.

By the fourth hand of gin she was even able to laugh at his expression when she won.

"You're lethal," he said with some feeling. "And I've seen dealers in Vegas with less dexterity."

"I have two younger cousins who are fond of card games," Amanda told him. "Neither is of age yet, but

I have the sneaking suspicion that Samantha got an expert to show her how to deal—and she taught me."

Ryder eyed her thoughtfully. "How are you with trivia?"

"Are you by chance referring to that trivia game I found in the closet with these cards?"

"I was, yes."

"Well, if you feel brave . . ."

"Your cousins are fond of trivia too?"

"No. I just read a lot."

"I think I feel brave," Ryder said, and went to get the trivia game.

They opted not to use the gameboard, deciding that they would each simply use the dice to select the categories and collect tokens for correct answers. Whoever ended up with the most tokens would be the winner.

It was a relaxing game to play, and an informative one when two people were tentatively getting to know each other. They pulled the thick cushions off the couch and sat on the floor with the big coffee table between them and the fire burning brightly beside them. Nemo, clearly feeling left out of things, dragged his rug closer and sprawled out near Amanda, thumping his tail companionably against the floor whenever a remark was addressed to him.

"All right," Ryder said when Amanda had selected a category. "Brace yourself. What type of betting is used in horse racing?"

"Parimutuel."

"Damn. Take a token and roll the dice again."

She did, and he went on to the next card. "Who was Napoleon's first wife?"

"That's easy. Josephine."

He looked at her suspiciously but with a gleam of amusement in his eye. "Have you memorized these cards?"

"Are you kidding? Look how many there are. Tell him, Nemo. Tell him I'm playing fair. Besides, I'm bound to miss one. Sooner or later." She took another token and rolled the dice again.

Ryder studied another card. "This is a good one. What does a nihilist believe in?"

Amanda frowned, working it out in her mind. "A nihilist? Nihilist. Annihilate. To destroy completely, to—nothing. He believes in nothing."

"Maybe we should have stuck to gin," Ryder said ruefully.

She grinned at him and took another token. "Persevere. My next category is"—she rolled the dice— "sports. Not my strong suit."

He smiled evilly after looking at the card. "How many men does a Canadian football team field?"

She didn't have to frown this time. "Now, there you've got me. I haven't the faintest idea."

"Twelve. My turn."

His category was geography. Amanda read the question silently, then giggled. "If you can answer this, you're a better man than I am, Gunga Din. What's the principal language of Trinidad and Tobago?"

Ryder blinked. "English."

"Give the man a cigar."

"I'll take a token." He did, then rolled the dice. "The category is literature."

"And the question is: What writer was nicknamed Papa?"

"Hemingway."

"Oh, a literate soul. I had no idea."

"Don't scoff. Bite her, Nemo. The next category is—entertainment. Question?"

"What symbolized justice and law to the Lone Ranger?"

" 'Who was that masked man,' " Ryder murmured almost as if by rote, then added, "A silver bullet."

Amanda tried not to think about masks. "At least you aren't gloating," she said.

"I'll do that later. When I win."

She made a rude noise and went on to the next question. Ryder answered that and another one successfully, but was baffled by how many feet apart the stakes were for men's horseshoe pitching. Forty.

Amanda was momentarily puzzled by the question asked her, but only because her answer didn't seem to make sense. "The difference between two square miles and two miles square is—two square miles. That is—I mean, two miles square is—is actually four square miles, so the difference is two square miles."

Ryder looked at the card in his hand and nodded slowly. "Well, you're right. I'm not quite sure how you got there, but the correct answer is certainly two square miles."

"I could draw a diagram," she offered solemnly.

"No. Thank you, but no. There are some mysteries in life destined to remain so."

Amanda nodded. "Me and the sphinx. The next category is geography. Read on."

"Where's the Sea of Tranquility?"

"No earthly boundaries in this game, I see. It's on the moon. 'Tranquility Base here. The eagle has landed.' "

"It's funny how we remember some phrases so well, isn't it?" he remarked, reaching for the next card.

"I think it's because we learn by rote," Amanda said consideringly. "We learn to connect things to other things. The moon landing. Pearl Harbor."

" 'A day that will live in infamy.' " Ryder nodded. "You may be right. Ready for the next question?"

"Shoot."

"Who painted the Sistine ceiling?"

"An easy one. Michelangelo."

"Okay. What does TKO stand for?"

"Technical knockout." Amanda smiled suddenly. "I'm not totally dumb about sports. I just know a few select things." And she proved that by correctly stating that the two categories of harness racing were pacing and trotting. She had, however, no idea that there were two heads on a croquet mallet. "They have heads?"

"It says here they do." Ryder looked faintly baffled himself, but picked up the dice for his turn.

Amanda watched him, feeling relaxed and comfortable. But then he looked at her, and she was instantly conscious of the electricity arcing between them. Hastily she reached for the cards. "Um . . . what travels in gaggles?"

"Geese."

He felt it too, she knew. It was in his voice, an almost imperceptible roughening, a suddenly husky note. That intensity creeping back. They couldn't ignore the strange awareness for long, either of them. She realized that. It was unnerving—and exciting. All her senses felt almost painfully alive, sensitive to everything around her in a way they'd never been before.

The lightness of the game was only an interlude. An area of calm between recognition and completion. But it was like the eye of a vast storm, with raw turbulence visible all around, a tangible force that could never be contained.

"Amanda?"

Quickly she reached for the next card. "The category?"

"Geography," he said after a moment.

She kept her gaze fixed on the card she held. "What country would you have to visit to see the ruins of Troy?"

"Turkey. I think."

"You think right. Next?"

The intensity receded. But it didn't vanish. It hovered close, on the edge of awareness.

Ryder was able to answer correctly that the swallows were supposed to return to the San Juan Capistrano mission every March 19, and knew that the last major league baseball player to bat .400 was Ted Williams, but he didn't know that the one thing in India you were forbidden to fly an airplane over was the Taj Mahal.

Amanda knew that a ring-shaped coral island was better known as an atoll, but couldn't remember that Sherlock Holmes's landlady was Mrs. Hudson. She got her turn back quickly, however, since Ryder didn't know that the only mammal with four knees was the elephant.

"Four knees?" he demanded skeptically.

"Says here."

"I knew that giraffes didn't have vocal cords, but I didn't know elephants had four knees."

Amanda suddenly recalled a circus visit years before. "Their back legs bend backward at the joint instead of forward. All four legs bend the same way. So they have four knees."

"Or four reversed elbows." Ryder blinked and seemed to consider what he'd said. "Two knees and two reversed elbows?"

"Reversed elbows?" Penny said, coming into the room with a tray. "What on earth—?"

Looking up at Penny solemnly, Amanda said, "Elephants have four knees. Or two knees and two reversed elbows. Ryder was trying to decide."

Penny put the big tray down on the coffee table beside the game board. The tray held coffee and sandwiches. "I think," she said in a conversational tone, "you two can definitely stand a little fuel for your systems. They seem to be operating at something less than full throttle."

"I resent that," Ryder said to her.

She eyed him. "I'm not surprised."

Amanda intervened hastily. "Is Sharon back yet?"

"No. I just called into town to check. They got there all right. But they won't be heading back this way until the storm's passed. Jake says even with the four-wheel-drive they found it rough going. The worst is supposed to be over within a couple of days, so they'll try then."

"Do we have enough supplies?"

Penny nodded. "Sure, for at least a week. And the bunkhouse has plenty. We'll be fine." She looked at Ryder again, and shook her head with exaggerated pity. "It's a shame for a mind to go. And you barely in your prime."

He returned her gaze very seriously. "Did you know," he said, "that you can't fly an airplane over the Taj Mahal?"

# *Six*

---

The storm raged, more or less, for two days. There were intervals of calm, but they never lasted long. The old house groaned and creaked in wind gusts of over forty miles an hour, and blowing snow was driven against the windows until it was almost impossible to see anything else.

They kept a fire going all the time in the den fireplace, mainly because the furnace went out twice. The first time it happened, Amanda went down into the basement and spoke sternly to it, adding a well-placed kick for emphasis.

"A furnace," Ryder told her severely, "is a piece of machinery, not a stubborn human."

"It worked, didn't it?" Amanda retorted.

They both listened to the soft roar of an undeniably working furnace, and Ryder was forced to admit that her tactics had accomplished their objective.

When the heat went off on the second day, it was

Ryder who unearthed a tool kit left by some of the workmen and descended into the basement.

"It's an electric furnace," he told Amanda and Penny in the kitchen as he was preparing to go down. "My business is electronics, after all."

Amanda, who had a strong feeling that electric furnaces were somewhat different from electronic games and computers, ventured to say, "Are you sure you know what you're doing?"

"It's just a piece of machinery," he said, and gave them both a step-to-one-side-you-peasants look as he picked up the toolbox and turned away.

They watched him disappear down the stairs to the basement. Amanda glanced at Penny. "What do you think?"

"I think we'd better bring in more wood and keep the fire going. Just in case. The wind's dropped for the moment, and Nemo needs to go out anyway."

Feeling slightly guilty at doubting Ryder's electronic expertise, Amanda nonetheless shrugged into her coat to go help bring in wood. She told herself firmly that it wasn't Ryder she was doubting, not really. It was just that the furnace had baffled men who specialized in furnaces.

So they brought in wood and added some to the fire in the den. All the rooms not in use had been closed off, the furnace vents shut so that all available heat would be concentrated in the occupied parts of the house. Ryder had repacked his things and moved to a second-floor bedroom near Amanda's so that they could close off the entire third floor.

"Now I've got a shower curtain," he had said gravely.

Amanda had managed not to look too guilty about the room she'd first assigned him, and had merely asked if there were enough blankets on his bed.

That had been the night before. Now, helping Penny fix supper in the big, warm kitchen, she listened to the increasing wail of the wind outside and, occasionally, a curse that floated up the steps from the depths of the basement. There were a good many bangs and thumps as well.

Amanda went down a half hour later to take Ryder a cup of hot coffee, but returned rather hastily, trying to smother giggles.

"Not just a piece of machinery after all?" Penny murmured with a smile.

"He says it's got gremlins in it," Amanda explained in a shaking voice. "At least I *think* that's what he said . . . with all the other descriptive words deleted."

Penny looked reflective. "I like a man who doesn't mind getting his hands dirty. Or is he?"

"Oh, definitely. And not just his hands. He had a smudge of oil or something across his nose." That sentence prompted another thought, and she added, "Is the hot water heater okay?"

"So far."

They worked together companionably for some time, both listening to the noises from the basement. Then there was a long silence. They looked at each other speculatively and waited. A couple of minutes later there was a final ringing thud—and the furnace started up.

Amanda looked at the basement door and waited. When Ryder came through it, she kept her face expressionless with an effort. He looked, she thought, like the survivor of a war fought against a very greasy army.

"I," he said with exquisite control, "want a shower."

Penny eyed him, then said mildly, "Supper's almost ready. Don't dawdle."

When he was almost at the hall door, Amanda said gravely, "Ryder? How'd you fix it?"

He half turned to give her a goaded look. "I kicked it," he said bitterly.

He was in a better mood by the time he got cleaned up and ate. In fact, Amanda thought later, he was a very even-tempered man. She glanced up from the book in her lap, taking the opportunity to study him since he seemed engrossed in his own book.

They were both sitting on the couch in the den, Amanda curled up like a cat in one corner with her stocking feet half tucked under a faded old gingham pillow. It was becoming a habit to end up in the den and read in the hours before they turned in for the night.

Penny, whose rooms were on the ground floor near the kitchen, watched television in her sitting room each evening; she'd said nothing about it, but it was fairly obvious that she was taking pains to leave them alone together as much as possible.

Not that very much happened, Amanda reflected, unsure if she was glad or bothered by that. The awareness between them hovered, occasionally creeping nearer at odd moments, but Ryder had made no effort to take advantage of it. Other than very casual and somewhat offhand touches, he kept his distance, and if that was difficult for him he didn't show it.

He was, she admitted, silently, a surprisingly comfortable companion. He was shrewd as well as intelligent, humorous, and appeared completely satisfied to play a game of cards or trivia or to read a book in her company.

She looked at him, not thinking very much now. Outwardly he was the prince of fairy tales—tall, dark, and handsome. Inwardly, of course, he was as complex as real people always were, filled with shades and layers. She was just beginning to know the inward man, beginning to recognize his mood by the tone of his voice, the set of his lips, or the shade of his eyes.

*I've stopped falling,* she realized suddenly. *I've landed. Landed in love.*

The phrase was peculiarly the right one. She felt as if she had indeed been falling, breathless and half frightened, the drop ending with a sudden thud that was definite. And that was, she thought, the way love happened. One fell over the edge of caution, helpless to stop it, bewildered by the inevitable force of the thing.

And landed.

It had been a long time since she had thought she was in love, and that had felt different. More—what? More dreamy, more complacent. At nineteen, falling in love brought complacency, the gratification of knowing that you were just like everyone else, about to become one of a pair, half of a couple. The reassuring knowledge that you were walking steadily down the right path of life.

Filled with expectations.

It was different, she thought, at twenty-eight. Complacency had become uncertainty. There were many paths, no "right" one, and all of them bumpy. There was the memory of pain, of shattered illusions, and the awful knowledge that people could hurt each other so dreadfully, especially lovers.

Amanda looked at him and told herself fiercely to expect nothing this time. To be grateful for his desire that was for her and not her possessions. To let herself feel these unfamiliar, exciting feelings without the murky shadow of expectations hanging over her.

Ryder looked up suddenly, meeting her gaze, and his own eyes were dark. He knew, she realized, that she'd been watching him. He had felt it.

"The book's not holding your attention?" he murmured, the lurking intensity in his voice now.

She managed what she knew was a strained smile. "No. I've already guessed whodunit." They were both reading—or had been reading—murder mysteries.

He continued to look at her for a long, steady moment. Then, very deliberately, he closed his book and leaned forward to place it on the coffee table. He took hers from her suddenly nerveless fingers and placed it there as well. Then he got to his feet and grasped her hands to pull her up.

"Ryder—" She didn't know what she was going to say, but a gentle finger over her lips stopped the unformed words.

In a casual tone with only a hint of tension, he said, "I think this has gone on long enough, don't you?"

She couldn't answer with words. His mouth covered hers, parting her lips with insistent demand, and the thrust of his tongue made the strength flow out of her legs in a rush. She felt herself lean into him, her body instinctively seeking his, and her arms slid up around his neck. The sudden explosion of heat inside her burned intensely, jerking a moan from her throat and making her shudder.

His deep, shattering kisses were a kind of possession, stark and raw, bringing all her senses vividly alive. The arms around her held her tightly, but she moved to be closer, fitting herself more intimately into his hardness. Her aching breasts flattened against the solid expanse of his chest, and she stood on tiptoe in an effort to be even closer as the burning hunger inside her flared.

An odd, rough sound escaped Ryder as he raised his head at last. Without a word he lifted her completely into his arms and carried her from the den. It occurred to Amanda vaguely to tell him that she was perfectly capable of walking, but the point didn't seem that important. She'd never been carried in a man's arms before, and was both surprised and disturbed at how vulnerable it made her feel.

Her weight seemed not to bother him at all as he carried her up the stairs to the second floor and her bedroom. The lamp on the nightstand was burning; she'd left it on when she had gone earlier for a book. The room was warm. Ryder closed the door behind them with a kick and carried her to the side of the bed before setting her on her feet. But then, pausing only to strip the covers back, he lifted her again and lowered her to the bed.

Amanda didn't try to deceive herself into believing she wasn't eager for this. For him. She loved him and she wanted him, and nothing else seemed to matter. Her arms went around his neck as he joined her on the bed, her mouth instantly responsive to the hunger of his.

He kissed her in that slow, shattering, absorbed way, as if lovemaking were only that, as if it were a completion instead of a preliminary activity. There was a dim astonishment in her that something she had always thought relatively simple and casual could, with Ryder, be so overwhelming.

But it was only a prelude, a beginning, and the building desire in them both demanded more. Ryder's lips left hers at last to move slowly down her throat, and one hand began unfastening the buttons of her flannel shirt. The heavy material was swiftly opened, the shirt somehow pushed off her shoulders and tossed aside. She felt his warm, hard fingers slipping beneath her back to unhook her bra, and then that was gone as well.

Ryder had been struggling to hang on to his control, but when the scrap of lace covering her breasts was gone he very nearly lost it. She was beautiful, just as he'd known she would be, and the sight of her round, firm breasts, the pink nipples tight and hard, sent a jolt of pure hunger through him. He lowered his head and drew one hard bud into his mouth while his hand moved to surround the other breast, his thumb rasping gently over the nipple beneath it.

Amanda gasped wordlessly, her body arching in a helpless response. The shock of pleasure was instant, spreading outward from deep inside her in ripples of sensation that stole her breath and clouded her mind. All her conscious awareness was focused on what he was doing to her. The erotic suction of his mouth was a caress that her body responded to with a wildness she couldn't begin to control. She was burning and couldn't be still, her head moving restlessly, her legs shifting, pressing together in an instinctive attempt to ease the throbbing ache that kept getting worse, stronger, until she thought she'd go mad with the awful tension.

She was so wrapped up in the sensations, so totally involved in her awakened body, she automatically lifted her hips when he unfastened her jeans and pulled them and her panties off.

"Amanda." Her name was a husky murmur, and his hot gray eyes were fixed, intent as he looked at her.

Caught in the desperate hunger he aroused in her, Amanda reached for the buttons of his shirt, frantic to tear away the last barriers between them. He helped her, his movements as jerky as her own. Clothing was thrown to the floor carelessly, blindly. When he was as naked as she, Amanda felt a primitive stab of excitement, a jolt at the realization that he was beautiful.

His power when clothed had been an understated thing, more a matter of broad shoulders and lithe grace than of muscular strength. But the muscles were there, hard and well-defined, rippling under his bronze skin with every movement he made. His broad chest was covered with a mat of thick black hair that arrowed over his flat stomach.

He was big and strong, his lean face taut and his eyes blazing with a hungry fire. She thought dimly that it would be easy to be afraid of his stark male power, to be wary of his unhidden need. But her own need was alive in her, and she felt no fear.

Ryder moved one hand to her quivering stomach and rubbed gently while his mouth caressed her breasts. He felt her fingers dig into his shoulders, heard the shaken moan of pleasure escape her, and another thread of his control snapped. She was so responsive . . . No barriers now, no elusiveness. The fire in her almost burned him, but he held his own raging desire in an iron grip.

There was something more than desire driving him, and he was dimly aware of it. Something almost primal, a fierce need to bind her to him in some immutable way so she would unquestionably belong to him. He didn't probe that need, he just accepted it. This was the way it had to be between them, an instinctive obedience to a force beyond knowledge or understanding.

This was *right.*

He couldn't get enough of her, couldn't stop touching her, learning her. His hand slid lower over her belly, settling over the soft copper curls and probing very gently.

Amanda thought she might have stopped breathing because there was no room in her lungs. She was filled with ragged tension screaming in every nerve ending. She felt his touch, and her own fingers gripped his shoulders frantically as her body responded wildly. Instinct demanded that she open herself to him, and with a shudder her body obeyed as her legs parted. She felt a burst of raw, hot pleasure as he stroked her gently, and a moan jerked from her throat. The fire inside her was burning out of control, and she couldn't hold herself still, couldn't think, couldn't do anything except give in to the blind, primitive drive toward release.

It seemed to last an eternity, tension spiraling until she could hardly bear it, until it seemed her body couldn't possibly contain the force of it, and then her senses shattered. A cry tore from her lips as pleasure washed over her in throbbing waves. She was hardly aware of the gasping sobs that escaped her as she lay trembling in the stunned aftermath of that explosion.

Her eyes opened slowly, almost blind at first but then focusing on his taut face. And the ebbing tension began building again. Now she was conscious of an empty ache inside her, a hunger for him that hadn't been satisfied. The searing heat of his kiss sent wildfire rushing through her.

He widened her legs and moved between them, still kissing her deeply. His hands were stroking her body, hard but gentle. Very slowly he eased into her, lifting his head to look down at her. He heard the sharp intake of breath, saw her eyes widen and then seem to lose focus, to go soft and dreamy and absorbed. It was the most wildly arousing thing he'd ever seen in his life, sending a jolt of pure raw craving through him.

He groaned harshly, half closing his own eyes as she lifted her hips tentatively to take more of him. His entire body was aching, rigid as he fought the urge to bury himself in her. This slow possession was tearing him apart, but it was an unbelievably sweet agony. Her body accepted his with silken heat, sheathing him completely as he pushed slowly inside her.

"Ryder," she murmured throatily, her arms around his neck now as her body cradled his fully.

Ryder gritted his teeth as a hoarse sound rumbled in his chest. The threads of his control were snapping, urgency building in him until he could no longer fight it. Almost frantically he began moving, feeling her take fire again. She was holding him, her soft little cries and throaty moans deepening his own taut pleasure. The strain of having held himself back so long had him on the ragged edge of exploding until rawly sensual tremors like nothing he'd ever felt before rippled along his spine.

He was deep inside her when the hot inner contractions of her pleasure caught him wildly in a stark caress, and he heard her wordless whimper even as a rasping groan tore free of him and his own tension snapped with a blind intensity that shuddered through him.

Amanda came back to herself with the small, stunned feeling of someone who had totally lost control for the first time in her life. It wasn't an unpleasant feeling, but definitely an unfamiliar one. She considered it briefly, then pushed it away to be dealt with, if necessary, later. In the meantime, she also felt totally exhausted, completely boneless, and warmly happy.

Ryder moved suddenly, rolling over so that she

was on top of him. "What took us so long?' he murmured, his voice still a little husky.

Amanda felt vaguely shy as she returned his gaze, but the expression on his face was both reassuring and slightly annoying. She didn't know which emotion to choose. He looked utterly satisfied, more than a little arrogant, and quite definitely possessive.

She cleared her throat softly. "My fault?"

"Well, you told me to slow down. Scruples," he said in a considering tone, "can be hell, can't they?" Then, without giving her a chance to answer, he added, "Are you coming back to Boston with me?"

Amanda blinked. Hope rose in her, but she pushed it back down fiercely. He hadn't said a word about caring for her, she thought, so it wasn't entirely clear what he meant by that question. Nothing to encourage hope. "Why do you ask?" she ventured.

Ryder moved again so that she was lying on her back beside him while he raised himself on one elbow. A slight frown drew his brows together, and his eyes became very intent. "Why do you think? Because I'm due to leave here in a little over a week."

Determined never again to be shattered by unfulfilled expectations, Amanda had very carefully not allowed herself to think of the future. Resolutely she clung to that decision. It was safer. "I have a job to do here, you know," she said mildly.

"Are you suggesting one of us commute?" he asked in a dry tone.

"That wouldn't be very practical."

"Then my money's on Boston. Amanda, I have a company there. So do you."

She shivered unconsciously, more uneasy than

cold, but Ryder immediately drew the covers up over them both.

"Amanda?"

What, she wondered, did he want from her? Did he want her in Boston so that they could spend an occasional night or weekend together? A nice, sensible, adult arrangement, with no ties or promises on either side?

Her mind shied violently at that. Maybe she could manage to be casual about this, not to cling to him, but she doubted her control if they became weekend lovers. But she couldn't tell him that without confessing her love, and she couldn't do that. He hadn't asked for her love, and it was still too new and vulnerable to be offered up carelessly.

She saw his eyes narrow at the long silence, and managed a slight smile. "Do we have to decide this right away? You aren't leaving tomorrow."

Ryder gazed down at her, conscious that his own feelings didn't make sense. She was his, she belonged to him, and he fully intended to make her accept that. Yet he didn't want to ask himself why, and he didn't want to look beyond that fact. He wanted her with him. Period.

His need for her to be at his side was as strong as the sexual desire still was, consuming him until he couldn't think past it. He slid one hand over her soft stomach, then moved it up slowly until his fingers closed gently over her full breast. He watched her face, seeing her eyes widen. He let his thumb brush very gently over her hardening nipple, and watched color bloom in her cheeks.

She cleared her throat. "Um . . . are we having the same conversation?"

"Uh-huh," he murmured, enjoying the feel of her warm flesh in his hand and very aware of his instant response to touching her. "Why do you think I want you with me? I can't keep my hands off you. The next week or so isn't going to be enough. Not nearly enough."

Amanda tried to think of something light and flippant to say, but her mind was moving sluggishly. Her body had forgotten exhaustion, responding instantly to his touch, and a feverish wave of desire swept over her.

"Ryder, you're not being fair."

"Who cares about fair," he muttered, pushing the covers down so that she was bare to the waist. He bent his head, his mouth seeking the warm curve of her breast.

She felt herself reaching for him, probing the muscles of his shoulders and back with her fingers. Her nerves were on fire already, her senses swimming with desire. She felt herself sinking into a swirling rush of hunger, and abandoned herself to it mindlessly.

It was very early when Amanda slipped from the bed the next morning. Even though the room was very bright because of the snow outside, a glance at the clock on her nightstand told her it was only a little after six. She was careful not to wake Ryder, although he was sleeping deeply and it didn't seem likely he'd be easily awakened.

Not after last night.

Their clothing lay tangled on the floor near the bed, a jumble of material. She picked up his things and left them on the bed, then put her own things aside. She got clean underwear from the drawer of her dresser and went into the bathroom, closing the door softly behind her.

She didn't let herself think very much until she stood under the shower, and even then her thoughts were disjointed. She felt so different. Her muscles were a little sore, and with every movement she was unnervingly conscious of a faint tenderness deep inside her. It had been a long time for her, and even though Ryder had been very gentle the first time, their subsequent joinings had proven to be considerably more . . . abandoned.

He hadn't hurt her at any time, but Amanda still felt dimly astonished that his need had been so potent—and that hers had matched his. Something so fiery, she thought numbly, had to burn out eventually. Didn't it? But it hadn't, at least not last night. Every time he had touched her, every time she'd met his darkening gaze, desire had flared between them like something alive and hungry.

Whoever had stated so firmly that male sexuality peaked in the late teens or early twenties, she thought, ought to have included Ryder in the study.

The thought was worrying, and she let herself worry about it. Her own desire sprang from love, but what about Ryder's? According to rumor, he'd had women chasing him for years; why did he want her so intensely? She knew she was attractive, but she was certainly no seductress and wasn't at all accustomed to inspiring violent passions in a man.

Granted, he could well be an extremely virile man with strong sexual appetites, she thought. That would explain his passion. And maybe it had been some time since his last . . . affair.

Having convinced herself of the likely source of Ryder's desire for her, she felt depressed. But before she could dwell on the painful thoughts, she felt a draft of cool air and turned hastily to find that Ryder had joined her in the shower.

"Good morning," he said, and pulled her wet body into his arms.

When Amanda woke for the second time that morning, it was to the smell of coffee and the somewhat muzzy thought in her mind that studies of male sexuality had no validity whatsoever. She was lying on her stomach, sprawled, actually, and she decided that somebody was going to have to build a fire under her to get her out of the bed.

"Have some coffee," Ryder's voice invited her.

With a concentrated effort she managed to roll onto her side and then her back. Once moving, it was somewhat easier to sit up against the pillows and pull the covers up to her breasts. She pushed her hair out of her eyes. There was a blur sitting on the edge of the bed. Automatically she brought her fingers to her eyes and rubbed gently, easing the morning dryness of her contact lenses.

"Have I given you a headache?" he asked.

"No. Contacts. They're dry in the morning." She brought her hands down and blinked owlishly several times, until the blur became him sitting on the bed. He had coffee. She accepted a cup gratefully. "Thank you."

"It's after nine," he offered.

"I'm not surprised." She wouldn't have been surprised if it had been after noon. Or even the next day. What did surprise her was that she had been carried into this room less than twelve hours earlier. She sipped the hot coffee and studied him with the detachment that comes of being just marginally awake. He had shaved, she saw, and was more or less dressed in jeans and an unbuttoned shirt. His mouth twitched suddenly, and she studied that with faint interest.

"You look beautiful in the morning," he said gravely.

Amanda didn't believe the gravity, because she'd seen the twitch. She half lifted her coffee cup in a vague salute. "Thanks awfully."

"You don't believe me?"

"I don't have to look into a mirror," she said, "to see what I look like. My hair was wet when I fell asleep, so I'm willing to bet it's a tangled mess. I'm always pale in the morning, and my eyes don't want to focus until the contacts stop being dry. And dammit, Ryder, stop smiling."

He couldn't help it. The "tangled mess" she'd referred to tumbled around her small face in waves of fire, more brightly red than usual against her creamy skin. And maybe she was a bit pale, but her skin was almost translucent. As for her eyes, they were huge and greener than they could possibly be, heartbreaking eyes—unfocused or not.

But instead of debating her beliefs, he said, "You were much more awake a few hours ago."

"My shower got invaded. I remember it distinctly."

"I told you I couldn't keep my hands off you," he reminded her solemnly.

Still not entirely awake, she said in an aggrieved tone, "Yes, but you were *asleep*. And I thought you'd sleep for a long time. You should have."

"I woke up, and you were gone. I just went looking for you. Is it my fault that I found you in the shower, all naked and slippery?"

Amanda blinked. She took a careful sip of her coffee, trying to wake up. "I'm curious about something," she said. "Are you this—well, intense—about all your bedmates?"

He leaned over to rest an elbow on the bed near her knees, as if he were fully prepared to stay awhile. "Are you asking about the women in my past?" he inquired politely.

"No." She reflected, then added, "Not specifically. I'm just wondering if it's a habit with you to be so—um—passionate." Her voice rose somewhat on the last word, as if it weren't quite the one she wanted.

"Does it bother you?" he asked softly.

Amanda looked at him and, finally, woke up. "No. How could it? You make me feel very wanted. I guess I'm just wondering why, that's all."

"Take another look in that mirror." She didn't, he realized, quite believe him. But she accepted it, half smiling and dropping her gaze to the cup in her slender hand. He didn't quite believe it himself.

Yes, she was certainly beautiful. He found himself realizing that often. She was beautiful, and he enjoyed watching her. But a hunger for surface beauty was a fleeting thing, so he knew his need for her didn't come from that. He knew her better after these last few days, and liked the quickness of her mind and the music of her laugh.

But a hunger as intense as the one he felt for her couldn't be triggered by a quick mind or a laugh. It was deeper than that. Primitive. It was a wordless thing inside him, a compulsive thing without knowledge.

Suddenly driven by that thing, he said, "No, Amanda, it isn't a habit with me."

She looked at him quickly, hearing the seriousness in his voice but wondering why he was frowning. Amanda felt as if he and she were swimming in something with undertows ready to pull them into dangerous depths. She wondered with a leap of hope if he might love her just a little.

Mildly she said, "I'm glad. A woman likes to know she's—unique. At least as long as it lasts."

His eyes narrowed. "You don't think it will."

Amanda kept her voice casual. "I don't believe in expectations, remember?"

Ryder stared at her for a long moment. Then in a rough voice he said, "Live with me."

# *Seven*

Amanda kept her gaze on her coffee, wondering how many other women had heard that . . . what? Invitation? Command? Whatever his past relationships, he had managed to keep them out of the gossip columns. Not that it mattered, not really. Her heart was urging her to accept whatever he offered, and living together was more than she had expected.

No, she thought fiercely, she hadn't *expected* anything. Not anything at all.

"Amanda?"

She looked at him and smiled slightly. "We can talk about it later, can't we?"

"Why can't we talk about it now?"

She shook her head. "Ryder, this has all happened very suddenly. Maybe that isn't unusual for you, I don't know, but it is for me. I just need a little time to get used to it, all right?"

The slight frown remained on his face, but he

nodded slowly. "All right. For the record, though, it is unusual for me. And I've never asked a woman to live with me before."

He hadn't, and he'd always thought the reason was basically a resentment about personal demands. He'd always been adept at compartmentalizing his life, and while the social compartment had certainly held women, he had never felt tempted to share his personal life with any one of them.

Now . . . He looked hard at Amanda. He knew he wanted her in his house, a constant part of his life. She returned his gaze, her feelings not showing on her face.

"I'll keep that in mind," she said lightly.

He wished he knew what she was thinking. Wished he knew why even now, she was holding him off just enough so that he was conscious of a distance between them. Trying to bridge that distance, he reached out his free hand and placed it gently over her stomach. His fingers probed almost obsessively to find the yielding firmness of her through the blankets.

"There is something we should talk about, though. A little late, maybe, but . . . I haven't been thinking very clearly since we met. I'm sorry."

Amanda glanced down at the big hand covering her stomach possessively. "Birth control? It's all right. I'm on the pill. Medical reasons." She wasn't sure why she added the explanation, except perhaps that she didn't want him to believe she'd been prepared to acquire a lover.

His eyes darkened with quick concern. "Medical? Is there something wrong?"

"No, not really. I have a very slight hormonal imbalance. A temporary thing, the doctor said. He'll probably want to take me off the pill in another few months. For that reason, I mean."

After a moment Ryder said, "If he does want to take you off them, we'll do something else."

"Sure," she said agreeably, still determined to expect nothing. He clearly believed they'd still be lovers some months from now, but Amanda refused to look past that day. Still, it bothered her that he kept referring—directly or indirectly—to a future for them. It was an oddly possessive attitude for a man who didn't strike her as the possessive kind.

He'd said he wasn't usually this intense in his relationships, yet he had pursued her with single-minded determination since the day he'd arrived. He had made love to her hungrily for the better part of their first night and morning together, and looked at her now with the intentness of desire still in his eyes. He had asked her to live with him when, he said, he had never asked a woman to do so before.

His every action seemed to indicate a desire for some kind of commitment between them, and yet not one word of caring had passed his lips. He was watching her now with that odd absorption, the same way he had kissed her, made love to her, the intensity of him overwhelming.

"Penny says breakfast is ready," he murmured.

Amanda looked at him for a moment, trying half-consciously to keep some part of herself untouched by him, unaffected. "I suppose she knows?"

He smiled. "When I went down looking for coffee, she handed me two cups. Why?" he added abruptly, the smile fading. "Does it bother you that she knows?"

Now, why, she wondered with vague surprise, did *he* sound defensive about it? She kept her own voice mild. "Why should it? We're all over twenty-one, Ryder."

"I know. I just didn't want you to be upset about it."

Amanda looked at her coffee, and then carefully drained the rest of it. The methodical action kept her attention occupied so that she couldn't blurt out the question in her mind. But she couldn't help but wonder what he'd planned to suggest if she *had* been upset about it.

She leaned over to set the empty cup on the nightstand, and said, "If breakfast is ready, we'd better go down."

"Okay." But he didn't move, except to take his hand off her stomach.

She waited a few beats, then realized that he wasn't going to get up. He was waiting. Watching her. Amanda was not, and never had been, a shy woman, but his concentrated attention was very unnerving. She felt ridiculously self-conscious; especially ridiculous given the fact that this man certainly knew every inch of her body naked or clothed.

"I realize," she said carefully, "that for me to feel embarrassed is a bit absurd. After last night. And this morning. But that's the way I feel. I'm not used to dressing in front of a man."

"Good," he said.

"Well, don't sound so arrogant about it," she said in sudden annoyance.

A gleam entered his eye, and though it contained amusement, it also held something else. "Amanda, maybe your past lover—or lovers—liked sex in the dark and dressing in the bathroom, but I don't. Not with you." His voice had a bite in it.

She stared at him, feeling a little stunned. Her first impulse was to tell him that the "lover" in her past was quite definitely singular, but she was too surprised by what had sounded like jealousy in his voice to be able to explain that immediately. And before she could get the words organized in her head, he was going on.

"I won't let you shut me out of anything in your life, especially not in the bedroom."

Because she was perplexed by the intensity of his reaction to what was, after all, a fairly minor point, Amanda instinctively took refuge in mildness herself. "I can see you've never lived with a woman."

He frowned. "What do you mean?" There was still a taut note in his voice.

"Well, she probably would have taught you never to pick a fight first thing in the morning. She also would have exposed you no doubt to the knowledge that we girls have modesty drummed into us from infancy. For most of us, parading around in front of a man stark naked is something we have to get used to. Gradually. In spite of what's gone on in the bed."

After a moment he said, "Was I trying to pick a fight?"

"It sounded like it from where I'm sitting."

He eyed her speculatively. "Your past lovers, you mean?"

Amanda sensed a corner, and didn't want to get

backed into it. She felt as wary as she would have been in a cage with a full-grown tiger. "Look," she said slowly, "I've already told you that I'm not a morning person. I don't cope well with stress until I've been up and about for an hour or so. Right now I want more coffee, and breakfast."

"So we postpone the fight?"

"If that's what we were about to have, yes, I'd rather we did. Do you mind?"

"Do you always schedule your fights?" he countered.

"Only when they start first thing in the morning."

"Okay." And then, dryly, he added, "Don't lose our place."

"Not a chance." She gazed at him for a minute or so, then muttered, "Oh, hell," threw back the covers, and slid out of the bed.

Ryder leaned back on his elbow and watched her very deliberately. But he couldn't hold on to the anger, not when he looked at her. If she did indeed feel embarrassed, he thought, it certainly didn't show. She moved with the easy, flowing grace of a young cat, her naked body creamy pale in the brightness of the room. Her hair was a tumble of fire around her shoulders.

He felt the simmering hunger inside him flare up, his heart slamming rapidly in his chest as if there'd been some jolt to his entire body. And there had been. She was so beautiful he couldn't stop looking at her, so damn sexy he couldn't stop wanting her. The round firmness of her breasts made his mouth go dry, and the slight sway of her hips was the essence of female suppleness.

He watched her bend slightly to pull clothing from

the drawers of her dresser. Lord, he thought, even the curve of her back was erotic. He was shattering inside, coming apart just looking at her.

Then his gaze moved slowly to her face, and a flicker of renewed anger tangled with desire. She looked aloof, detached, as if she were alone in the room. But before he could react to that, she stepped to the bathroom door and sent him a smile.

A very sweet smile. And then she went into the bathroom and shut the door softly. The click of the lock was audible.

Ryder looked down at the remains of his cold coffee and reflected somewhat wryly that he had only himself to blame. He had pushed, and what little experience he'd had of her should have warned him that wasn't the way to go. Not with Amanda. When she was pushed, she either bristled or else retreated into a shell he hadn't been able to penetrate.

But she'd been so responsive in his arms, so utterly willing and passionate, he had assumed . . . what had he assumed? That the fight was over? That she belonged to him now, his to touch or kiss or watch whenever he damned well pleased?

Arrogant, she'd said. Maybe he was at that.

He had half expected her to be a bit shy with him after the tempestuous night before, but she hadn't been. Granted, she'd been a bit slow to completely wake up, the interim filled with her apparent surprise that he could feel such strong desire for her so soon again.

That was when it began to bother him. He had sensed the distance between them, her emotional aloofness, and it had been a curious, unwelcome jolt. She had neatly sidestepped the issue of them living together. She'd been casual about birth control, surprised that he'd thought she might mind Penny knowing about their relationship, and even more surprised when he had—he admitted it to himself—uttered a probing taunt about her past lovers.

She'd recognized that taunt for what it was, and had instantly retreated behind her mild shell. She'd shown no curiosity about his past affairs except in a very general way, and she was clearly unwilling to satisfy his about the men in her past.

Not, at least, until she'd had another cup of coffee.

Ryder didn't know why it was bothering him so much until he thought it through. He had never felt the slightest bit of jealousy or possessiveness over a woman. Until Amanda. But not knowing what lay in her past was deeply disturbing, because he didn't know how much it mattered to her even now. He knew she'd been hurt, but he didn't know how badly. He didn't know if her emotional distance with him was some defense or the natural response of a woman who had given her heart to another man.

Could she be so responsive to him physically if that other man was still in her life. In her heart?

He didn't want another man in her life . . . in her heart. He wanted her to think only of him, to be aware of him the way he was aware of her. He wanted her to snap at him if he made her mad, a gut-level response instead of that quick, careful retreat.

He wanted to *matter* to her.

She smiled at him when she came out of the bathroom, then went to the closet and slipped her feet into a pair of loafers, then turned to look at him with a questioning lift of her brows as she picked a brush up from the dresser and quickly restored order to her thick hair.

She spoke as if nothing at all had happened between them, he thought. She was wearing an emerald green sweater over jeans, looking very lovely. Her expression was calm, but there was a shadow of wariness in her eyes. Still looking at him, she reached for a tiny bottle of perfume and dabbed a bit absently on her throat and wrists.

"You going to lie there all day?" she asked briskly.

Ryder got off the bed slowly. He picked up her coffee cup, holding it with his own in one hand. "Well, certainly not alone," he said.

Without responding to that, Amanda walked to the door and opened it, automatically looking down to keep from falling over Nemo. Except he wasn't there. "Have you seen Nemo?" she asked as Ryder joined her in the hall.

"In the kitchen. Sulking."

"Why's he sulking?"

"Because," Ryder said, "I nearly broke my neck over him when I went to get the coffee. He was parked outside the door."

"Did he faint?"

Ryder rested his free hand on the small of her back as they went toward the stairs. He had to touch her, it was a compulsion. Whenever he was near her it was as if he couldn't help himself. "Yes. I caught myself apologizing to him when he came to, but he wasn't having any."

Amanda wanted to be amused about that, but all

she could think of was the possessive hand on her back. Until this morning she'd thought that Ryder's intensity came from building desire, that there would be less of it once they slept together, but she knew now there was more to it than that. Much more. Because he was even more intense than he had been. It was in his eyes, was an undercurrent in everything he said. It was in the proprietorial way he touched her and the intent way he looked at her.

She felt . . . *claimed.* She wasn't angry about that, since she was convinced it was a temporary thing. She just wanted to understand. But she couldn't ask him because asking would be implying the need to define boundaries, to agree on ground rules, to set up expectations.

"Are you taking Nemo back to Boston with you?" Ryder asked as they reached the bottom of the stairs.

She answered almost absently. "I don't know. I hadn't thought about it."

"There's plenty of room at my place for a big dog."

On the surface it was such an innocent comment, but Amanda's abstraction vanished. She didn't look at him as she said casually, "Then I'm surprised you don't have one."

"I was saving myself for you and Nemo."

The retort was almost funny, but she heard a note of frustration in his voice, and wasn't tempted to laugh. And she was very grateful that they reached the kitchen then, where they wouldn't be alone, where he would stop pushing.

Penny looked up as they came in, her expression as calm as always. "According to the weather reports, the storm's pretty much over. And the temperature's rising. Some of that stuff out there might even melt before the next storm system moves through."

"I liked being snowed in," Ryder said.

Amanda couldn't help watching him when she thought he wasn't looking. He drew her gaze like a magnet. It was taking every bit of control she could muster to keep a part of herself unaffected by him, separate from him. But she needed that distance for her own sanity. She loved him so much that holding it inside her was like pain, cutting her up. She wanted to reach out to him, to offer her love, to accept anything he had to give her.

She was afraid of losing emotional control. Afraid that her love would make her cling, make her assume things. Before, she had loved with recklessness of youth, with the blind faith in princes and happy endings.

But she wasn't reckless anymore. She didn't expect men to be princes, and she didn't expect happy endings.


"Ready to finish the fight?"

They were in the den, alone since Nemo had chosen to remain in the kitchen after breakfast. The worst of the storm did seem to be over, and only a light snow was falling outside while the wind had stopped. Amanda wandered over to the window and stood looking out, very conscious of the peculiar quiet that always wrapped a house when there was snow on the ground.

"No," she said finally.

"Why not?"

She half turned to look at him, feeling the coldness of the window against one arm. "Because I don't want to fight with you," she said.

Ryder was standing by the fireplace only a few feet away, watching her. He wanted to go to her, to take her in his arms so that she couldn't hold him away from her. He wanted that so badly his whole body ached. But the memory of last night kept him still. He could bridge the physical distance between them easily, and he knew it; she was too responsive to him to be able to hold him off that way.

He'd thought about it during breakfast, realizing finally that his taunt about past lovers had been more than just his worry about how much her past meant to her. It had also been a dig at the shell she had retreated into, an effort to close the emotional distance she had created.

Maybe passion would do that as well, at least while it was burning between them. But the problem with that was his own response. He could barely remember his name when he held her, no less manage to string a few words together and demand answers.

She shifted nervously as he stared at her, her eyes wary. His own gaze narrowed. He didn't like the idea that he made her nervous, but ignored the pang for the moment. If that was all he had, then he'd damned well use it to break through her shell. No matter what it cost him.

"Did those past lovers of yours like sex in the dark, Amanda? Dressing and undressing in another room? Did they let you pretend you'd never gone crazy in bed?"

She paled slightly, and a glint of green fire ignited in her eyes. "What is this, male-ego time? You want to know how you compare with your predecessors?"

There was nothing mild about her expression now, nothing guarded or careful in her words. That was a surge of pure temper, and Ryder didn't hesitate to keep throwing wood on the fire. "Well, if I'm the most recent in a long line, I'd really like to know it."

"My bedroom doesn't have a revolving door, dammit!" she snapped.

"No, but it's filled with ghosts, isn't it?"

She shook her head angrily. "Stop it."

"Was that why you backed off so quickly this morning? Was that why you didn't want to talk about living together, about any kind of future? Because you woke up with a man instead of one of your ghosts?"

"Stop it!"

"But it's just one ghost, isn't it, Amanda? Just one ghost you can't get out of your head."

"Yes!" She glared at him furiously. But then, as the satisfaction in his eyes registered, her anger died. He hadn't been accusing her of sleeping around, she realized slowly. And he hadn't wanted her to compare his prowess as a lover to any other man's. That had been a . . . a diversionary tactic. He'd chipped away at her guard, arousing her anger deliberately in order to get at the truth.

"One man," he said quietly. "One past lover. And it was a long time ago, wasn't it?"

Why was he doing this? She didn't understand why he wanted to know. But she couldn't retreat from his insistence, because he had stripped away something and there was nothing left for her to hide behind.

"What were those expectations of yours, Amanda? How did he hurt you?"

After a moment she went over to the couch and sat down. She didn't speak until he joined her. He didn't touch her, just sat about a foot away, half turned on the couch so that he could watch her.

"Ryder, I was nineteen. He isn't in my head anymore. I can barely remember what he looked like."

"That isn't what I meant, and I think you know it." Ryder hesitated, then said, "You don't expect anything at all from me, do you? Nothing. And I want to know why, Amanda."

"I don't expect anything from anyone." Her voice was tightening. "And I don't see why that should matter to you. It's my own business."

"Tell me."

She looked at him levelly. "All right. But telling won't change anything."

"Just tell me."

Amanda shrugged. "As I said once before, it isn't a particularly original story. I fell in love. It's easy to do when you're nineteen. Storybook stuff. We were going to get married. And live in an ivy-covered cottage with a rose garden and a white picket fence. I was that far gone," she added self-derisively.

Ryder felt an urge to reach out to her but kept himself still and waited.

She wasn't looking at him now. She wasn't looking at anything at all. "I think they ought to have mandatory high school courses in reality," she said softly, not at all derisive now. "Because it was right there in front of me all the time, and I didn't see it. I was in love, so I . . . I expected him to be in love. That was what hurt so much in the end. Not that he didn't love me, but that I had so blindly assumed he did. That wasn't his fault. It was mine."

"What happened?" Ryder asked.

Her smile was twisted. "You know what they say about eavesdroppers hearing no good of themselves. I heard him talking to a friend of his one day. He was bragging that he had me right where he wanted me. He said I'd do anything for him, anything at all. And he was right, that was what sickened me. He was right."

"Amanda—"

"I stood there, listening. And I couldn't believe what I was hearing. All that storybook stuff kept getting in the way, all those expectations. Even when I listened to him talking to his friend, carefully detailing his step-by-step plan to marry a fortune, I was making excuses for him. Because I couldn't bear to lose the dream that everything was perfect.

"But every word he said tore the dream away until there was nothing but reality left. And do you know, I was still willing to believe in him. I thought he could explain away that cold-blooded plan, convince me it was just a joke or something. So I confronted him."

"And he couldn't," Ryder said quietly.

"He didn't even try." Her voice was almost inaudible. "He was the one who was convinced. Convinced that I'd do anything for him. That I'd even marry him knowing the truth. He said we were a perfect match. That hurt most of all."

Ryder drew a hard breath. "So, no expectations. Keeping yourself emotionally detached."

She didn't look at him because she was afraid he'd somehow see that her "detachment" with him was only a lie she was clinging to. "Don't you see? If you expect nothing, you won't be disappointed."

"You let one bastard do that to you?"

Amanda rose abruptly from the couch because she had to move. She stood before the fire, looking down at the flames, aware that he had followed her. "I asked myself that in the beginning. So the next time I met a man I liked, I just tried to—well, expect a little less. But the end was the same."

"Was he a lover?"

"No. Nor the next man. I didn't want to be that vulnerable again."

Ryder put his hands on her shoulders and turned her to face him. "What about when I showed up?"

She looked at him and, very deliberately, said, "You didn't know who I was."

His jaw tightened. "So you could be sure I wanted you for yourself. But you let yourself be vulnerable again."

"No. Not this time. You were right. This time I don't expect anything at all. Why should I? You weren't using sex as a means to an end—sex *was* the end. And I wanted it too."

Ryder's hands tightened on her shoulders. In the same deliberate tone she had used, he said, "Live with me."

She wanted to lean against him, to put her arms around him and agree to anything if it meant being with him. The depth of her own love was terrifying. *I would have done anything for him.*

"Amanda, dammit—"

"Ryder, we can talk about that later."

He stared at her for a long moment and then said, "You're going to live with me, you know. I'll convince you."

Relieved that they were at least getting away from that other, painful subject, she managed a light tone. "Oh? Are you going to promise me hot and cold running maids who do windows? All the latest movies beamed into your house by satellite? A spectacular view?"

His lips curved slowly. "No."

"What, then?"

Ryder lifted her into his arms and strode toward the stairs. "A king-size bed," he said.

Amanda clutched at his neck. "What're you—"

"If you don't know, I wasted my time last night."

She didn't know whether to giggle or swear at him. He was so damned *overpowering*. Baiting her until she told him things she hadn't meant to reveal, listening without saying very much, and then telling her she was going to live with him. And now . . .

She couldn't pretend it was just sex, not when he touched her. He had to know there was more. She wanted to say it, wanted to tell him she'd never felt like this about any man, never felt so wildly. But he hadn't asked for her love, and she wasn't going to offer it.

As he reached the landing she cleared her throat and managed to say, "Ryder, it's almost noon—"

He gave her a fierce look as he carried her into the bedroom and kicked the door shut. "I know, it's indecent. You've got to stop throwing yourself at me like this."

Amanda might have come up with some retort to that very unfair remark, but Ryder set her on her feet and covered her lips with his before she could say a word.

He had her so off balance by then that she simply melted against him. His hands curved over her bottom to hold her tightly, kissing her the way he did, in that strange, focused way that was like gasoline thrown on a fire.

"No ghost this time," he muttered as he lifted his head. He caught the bottom of her sweater and pulled it quickly off. Her bra followed, and his hard hands surrounded the swollen curves of her breasts.

Amanda bit back a moan, trying to think. "There wasn't one before."

"Yes, there was."

"No. He—"

"Not *him*. What he left you with." Ryder's voice was low and hoarse, and he didn't pause in undressing her.

The heat filling her made thought impossible. Amanda gave up trying to understand what he meant. Her senses were reeling and her hands were shaking as she tried to help him get rid of their clothing. And when they fell together onto the bed, she was conscious of nothing but him.

"Some manager I am," she murmured in disgust a considerable time later.

"You're managing your guest just fine as far as I'm concerned," Ryder told her complacently, then uttered a faintly exasperated oath as she pulled away from him. "Where are you going?"

Amanda slipped from the tumbled bed and began dressing determinedly. She still felt a bit self-conscious but tried to ignore that. "Downstairs. I've heard the phone ring several times, and poor Penny's had to answer it. I told you I was here to work, dammit."

"We've been snowed in," he pointed out, linking his fingers together behind his neck as he lay and watched her dress. "There's been no work to do."

"There will be now. The storm's over, and they've already started clearing the roads. The work crew will probably be back tomorrow, and I've got to get the old office ready for them to paint."

Ryder frowned slightly. "So that means the other guests will be showing up."

"I suppose." Amanda went over to the dresser to run a brush quickly through her hair. Then, with the automatic habit instilled in her by her aunt, she touched a perfume stopper to her wrists and throat. "Unless some of them have canceled by now. That might be why the phone was ringing."

"All our beautiful solitude shot to hell. Come here."

She eyed him warily. "I don't think so."

"I just want a kiss," he said in an innocent tone.

Amanda tried to judge his mood. Playful, she decided, but the intensity was lurking. "Ryder, I'm just going downstairs, not out of your life forever. And you'd better head in that direction yourself if you want lunch."

"You aren't going to serve me in bed?"

"Fat chance."

He sat up abruptly. "Then come here and kiss me. It's the least you can do to keep a guest happy."

She found herself moving toward the bed, and wondered rather desperately if she was going to have any will left by the time he was through with her. He caught both her wrists and tugged gently until she bent down, then fitted his mouth to hers and kissed her thoroughly.

When Amanda was finally allowed to straighten up, she drew a breath and blurted out, "Lord, you're dangerous."

His eyes gleamed at her. "That's the nicest thing you've ever said to me."

She backed toward the door. "Don't take it as a compliment. I'm not sure I meant it that way."

Ryder swung his legs from the bed. "We should certainly make sure. I hate imprecise definitions."

The intensity wasn't lurking anymore. It was *there*. Amanda opted for discretion over valor, and beat a hasty retreat.

# *Eight*

Ryder sat on the side of the bed, looking blindly at the door. Something was nagging at him, and the feeling had been growing. There was something . . . something familiar. It was like a tune he knew the words to but couldn't remember. He drew a short, impatient breath, then went abruptly still.

Again. A sense of déjà vu too fleeting to grasp. Something he had heard before, or said before, or done . . . something. It came in a flash, a maddening sliver of knowledge, vanishing the instant he was aware of it. And it had something to do with Amanda.

He had the feeling that if he could only concentrate when he was with her, he'd have it. But when he was with her she filled his mind to the exclusion of all else.

He rose slowly and began to dress, trying to keep his mind blank and receptive. But the sliver of knowledge remained just out of reach.

When Ryder went downstairs a few minutes later, he found Penny at the counter in the entrance hall frowning down at a paper lying between her elbows. She had the air of someone waiting patiently, which roused him from his abstraction.

"What's up?" he asked as he reached the bottom of the stairs.

She looked at him. "I just thought I'd wait for Mr. Fortune to call. He's the only one who hasn't."

"Cancellations?"

"Yep. They hadn't bargained for full winter, just the edge of it. So they called in regrets and apologies. Everybody but Cyrus Fortune."

"I don't think he'll cancel," Ryder said absently. "Where's Amanda?"

She nodded toward the secondary hallway that ran behind the staircase. "In the office. She was looking for a ladder, and then—"

"A ladder?" He muttered a curse, and turned away before she could complete the sentence. He went quickly down the hallway, looking into two bare and empty rooms before he found the old office. There wasn't much in it, just a big steel desk pushed into the center of the room along with a couple of filing cabinets and uncomfortable-looking chairs.

And Amanda up on a ladder as she struggled to unhook a tremendous moosehead from the wall between two curtainless windows.

Ryder didn't waste any time, especially since the ladder looked treacherously unsteady. He went swiftly and soundlessly around the clutter of things in the center of the room, and firmly grasped the ladder on either side of Amanda's thighs.

"What are you doing?" he demanded.

She started and looked back at him. "Damn! Don't creep up on people like that. You scared me."

"I think this is where I came in."

"I didn't fall this time," she protested.

"Come down from there. You can't possibly wrestle with that trophy while you're on a rickety ladder."

Since she had already realized how heavy the moosehead was, Amanda was forced to agree with him. "I know," she said with a sigh. "But I want that thing down. I won't leave *any* house decorated with an executed animal."

He eyed the creature in question, which was a very large specimen of its kind. "I'll get it down for you," he said. "And you don't have to sound so hot about it. I don't really agree with the practice myself, and I certainly didn't shoot the beast."

"I should hope not."

"I shoot only stubborn redheads."

"With ladder fetishes?"

"Those are the ones."

"You know, I got along fine with ladders before you came along. I can't imagine how."

"Me neither. Get down."

She looked at the moosehead again and shuddered visibly in disgust. "The very idea of it," she muttered. "Hunting something that can't shoot back, and then hanging the poor thing on the wall. . . ."

Ryder had his hands on her waist now as she backed down the ladder, and that sensation of déjà vu swept over him again. Triggered, his memory worked. He suddenly recognized the words she had spoken . . . and what his senses had been telling him. And this time he got it.

The perfume. Dammit, her *perfume*. He'd been conscious of it only peripherally, as a part of Amanda, a soft, faintly spicy scent that was uniquely her.

Yet it was familiar, that was what had been bothering him. And it all made sense now. She had dropped into his arms from a ladder, and his desire for her had been so instantly aroused that he'd been baffled. He couldn't understand how he could feel so much, so swiftly, for a stranger.

Until Amanda fell into his arms, he'd been haunted by an enigma. She had danced with him, walked with him in a garden, melted in his arms. She had spoken of the things she was "for" and those she was against—*hunting anything that can't shoot back*. And she had talked about not believing in princes or happy endings.

And then . . .

Amanda taking fire in his arms. Seeming so elusively familiar that he had doubted his senses. Holding herself away from him emotionally with stubborn aloofness because she wouldn't allow herself to have expectations. Because the prince had seduced her and won her heart with the cold-blooded ruthlessness of ambition.

Amanda was Cinderella.

"Ryder?" She was looking up at him, puzzled. "Is something wrong?"

It was on the tip of his tongue to demand to know why she hadn't told him, but he swallowed the words. He had to think about this, had to understand why he was feeling a fierce sense of satisfaction, and an even greater anxiety.

"No," he said, "Nothing's wrong." He glanced at

the moosehead, then back at her upturned face. "Come to think of it, getting that thing down looks like a two-man job. Trust you to try and do it on your own."

"Well, but—"

He kept one hand on the small of her back as he ushered her firmly from the room. "We'll let the workmen worry about getting it down. Let's have lunch."

"Who elected you chief?"

"I did. The vote was unanimous. We're going to have lunch and help Penny clean up, and then we'll both do whatever it is you feel has to be done before the workmen get here."

"Why both of us? Ryder, this isn't your job."

"I want to be with you."

"How flattering."

She stole a glance up at his face. It was calm now, but in the office, for just an instant, he had looked strange. The expression had vanished too quickly for her to be able to identify it, but it bothered her.

She didn't have very much time to think about it during the remainder of the day. There really wasn't much to do in order to get ready for the returning workmen, but Ryder managed to keep her busy. He seemed to be in a peculiar mood, watchful and somehow withdrawn into himself more than was normal for him.

Amanda wondered if he was already tiring of her, but she was reassured on that score during the night. In fact, if anything, he was more passionate, more intense. So much so that it was late in the morning when she woke up.

Alone.

She could dimly hear sounds of activity in the house, and realized that the workmen had returned. She got up and dressed, wondering where Ryder was. When she went out into the hall, she discovered that Sharon had returned. Sharon was in her late teens, a bright, energetic girl who was taking a year off from college to earn some extra money. She was almost a head taller than Amanda, and very fair.

"Hi, Amanda. Did you like being snowed in?"

"It had its points," Amanda said with feeling. She sighed as crashes and thumps sounded in the house. "Silence, for one. When did you get back?"

"About an hour ago. We went by the airport to see if there were any stranded travelers bound for here, and since Mr. Fortune had just arrived we gave him a lift."

Amanda blinked. "You did?"

"Sure. He's the most amazing-looking man, Amanda. Like Santa Claus—but not fat at all. Just *big*. And he has the kindest eyes. Mr. Foxx has been showing him around."

Which explained, Amanda thought, Ryder's absence. "I see."

Cheerfully Sharon went on. "I'm going to strip the beds in the rooms we won't need. Do you want me to do anything to yours?"

"No, thanks. I've gotten used to taking care of it myself."

"Okay. See you later."

Amanda nodded rather absently, then went on toward the stairs. So Cyrus Fortune had been here for an hour, and Ryder with him. She wondered if the deal was wrapped up already. She was halfway down when she heard voices, and almost at the bottom when she caught the tail end of a conversation.

". . . really a splendid example, and a fine piece of work. I can recall outings with my father when I was just a boy. A long time ago, of course."

As they appeared from the direction of the secondary hallway, Ryder looked up and saw her. "Good morning, Amanda. This is Cyrus Fortune. Cyrus, Amanda Wilderman."

Her first impression of the man was sheer size. He was extremely large, and moved with surprising lightness and grace. He was also dressed completely in white, possessed a luxurious white beard, and had vivid but benign eyes. He was carrying a gold-headed cane, though he didn't seem to need it in order to get around.

"Miss Wilderman. A pleasure."

He also had a low, rich voice, elegant hands, and an utterly charming smile. And he was— No, she thought. Her memory had to be playing tricks on her. He couldn't have been the man at the ball, the one she'd run into as she was leaving. That was absurd.

"Make it Amanda, please, Mr. Fortune. Glad you finally made it."

"I've already explained the situation to Cyrus, Amanda." Ryder's voice was calm. "I've told him we're both going to make offers for the rights to the patent."

Shocked, she stared at him. "You told him . . ."

Fortune's bright eyes flicked from her pale face to Ryder's expressionless one. "I believe I'll go to my room and unpack," he said gently. "Ryder, thank you for showing me around. I'll see both of you later."

They watched him ascend the stairs with an ease that was surprising for a man of his bulk and age, and then Ryder looked at her. "Tactful, isn't he?"

"You told him—"

"All the privacy of a goldfish now," he murmured. "The den, or the bedroom?"

Amanda swung around on her heel and went into the den. She felt angry, a little bewildered, and more than a little uneasy. What had Ryder done? The room was empty, but there was no door to close to ensure privacy. She kept her voice low as she turned to face him.

"What was that all about?"

He looked mildly surprised. "I thought it was clear."

"*You're* here to talk to him about the rights. I'm not. I told you we weren't going to offer—"

"I know what you told me. I have a good memory. You sidestepped that, Amanda. Just the way you've been sidestepping any commitment to me."

She bit her lip, and concentrated stubbornly on the business problem. "Look, I told you we were going to sign Dunbar. We won't need the new system."

Ryder shook his head slowly. "Now, that," he said, "is bull. If you'd had the chance to bid on the rights without knowing me, without having been on the spot more or less by accident, you wouldn't have hesitated."

"Ryder—"

"The truth, Amanda."

She hesitated, then said, "All right, maybe I wouldn't have. But that doesn't mean—"

"I'll tell you what it means. It means you came down on the fence again, detached and safe. You took one look at a potential problem, and removed yourself with all speed to avoid it."

"I didn't want to take advantage of a fluke," she said tightly. "You came here to talk to Fortune, he offered you the first chance, and that was all.'

"Was it? Sure there wasn't a little bit of charity and self-preservation involved? I told you I had limited resources, that I knew the competition could outbid me easily. Was that when you decided to stay carefully out of it? To neatly remove yourself from the fight before it *became* a fight, because you were so sure I'd lose and you didn't want that on your conscience?"

"I'm not bidding," she said, the words evenly spaced and distinct.

He looked at her for a moment, then said flatly, "Amanda, I'll fight—or I'll walk away. But I will be *damned* if I'll win by default."

"Why?" Her voice was shaking now. "Why are you doing this?"

"Expectations," he said very softly. "It seems I'm the only one who has them in this relationship. And I do have them. I expect you to fight for what's best for you and your company. I expect you to have the strength and the courage to fight. I expect you never to take the easy way just because the other ways are tough. And I *expect* you to get the hell off that fence and take sides."

"Against you?"

If he hesitated, it was almost imperceptible. "In this case, yes. The ghosts are still there, Amanda.

You're afraid to risk anything. You won't risk your emotions with me; you won't risk *my* emotions in fighting me. You sit on your safe little fence and insulate yourself."

"I can't be your competitor *and* your lover!"

He took a half step closer but didn't touch her. He seemed a little pale to her, and his eyes were glittering in a way she'd never seen before. When he spoke, his voice was very soft. And cut like a knife.

"You aren't my lover, Amanda. Lovers risk. They make themselves vulnerable to each other. Remember what you said? What you so carefully explained? You didn't make yourself vulnerable to me. All I wanted was sex, you said, and that was fine with you. You could accept that . . . and expect nothing from me. We aren't lovers. We just sleep together."

Amanda wanted to lash out at him, to protest that *he* hadn't risked. But he had. Not his heart, but something. He'd asked her to live with him, had offered a commitment of a kind. And she hadn't been able to accept it.

She wondered, for the first time, and with a jolt, what her love was worth if it had to be hoarded, had to be wrapped in careful layers to protect it from harm. What would happen to it there, locked away in that dark, airless place? What would her love be if she was ever able to offer it to him?

Would it be worth having then? Or would it be something withered and dead?

It hurt to think that. It hurt dreadfully. The pain of shattered illusions and girlhood dreams had not been nearly so bad as this. Ryder's fence analogy had been apt, she realized bitterly. She'd avoided taking sides her entire adult life, sitting safely on a fence, wrapped in her detachment.

And when she had landed in love despite that, she had instantly sealed the feelings deep inside her, where he couldn't see them and she wouldn't have to deal with them. She had offered her desire because his was so intense, and she would therefore risk nothing.

She looked at him, and blinked because he seemed hazy. The mist cleared slowly. She felt curiously numb, thinking idly that his gray eyes were so intense they were almost silver, oddly fierce.

Tonelessly she said, "I can have the paperwork here by tomorrow afternoon."

"All right." He sounded a little hoarse, and cleared his throat quickly. "I'll tell Cyrus that we'll both submit sealed bids to him as soon as your paperwork's here."

She nodded.

Ryder seemed to hesitate for an instant, then turned and left the room.

Amanda walked slowly to the counter in the foyer and stood for a long minute staring at the phone. She was still fence-sitting, she realized. Risking nothing of herself. In fighting Ryder this way, she wasn't likely to lose. Not the business deal, at least.

She reached for the phone.


With the workmen back on the job, it was easy to stay busy for the remainder of the day. Amanda saw Ryder and Cyrus Fortune at meals, but otherwise occupied herself in other parts of the house.

But no matter how busy she made herself, she couldn't stop trying to sort through the tangle of emotions. She loved Ryder, yet she hadn't dared risk telling him, showing him. The desire between them was overwhelmingly intense, yet she hadn't dared assume that he felt something deeper than passion.

Once she had looked at a man with unshadowed trust, with blind certainty, and said, "I love you." It had felt so natural then, so simple. A fact, stated with assurance. An emotion confident of a matching response.

Because she had believed in princes then. And happy endings.

It would never be that easy again.

*I expect you to never take the easy way just because the other ways are tough.*

Dear Lord, was she such a coward? So wary of pain she wasn't willing to risk anything for love?

The questions went around and around in her head until she felt sick with the struggle to come to terms with them. She ate almost nothing at supper, conscious of Ryder's gaze on her but unwilling to meet it. As soon as she could decently slip away, she did, retreating to the solitude of her room.

She took a long shower and washed and dried her hair. She put on her prettiest nightgown, realizing suddenly that Ryder had never seen her in sleepwear. In the nights they'd spent together, she'd slept naked in his arms.

She prowled restlessly around her room, picking up a book and then putting it down, filing her nails. Nemo asked to be let in, but clearly sensed her tension and didn't remain long before asking to be let out again.

It was nearly midnight, the house quiet, when Amanda realized he wasn't going to come.

She crawled into bed and turned out her light.

"I didn't know anyone was still up."

Ryder looked around, a bit surprised himself to see Cyrus Fortune come into the den. The room was dark except for a dying fire in the hearth, and Ryder had been alone in there for several hours. He watched the old man move around the end of the couch and sit down before he spoke.

"I couldn't sleep." He felt peculiarly comfortable with Fortune, and had from the beginning, a rare occurrence in his experience.

"Troubles of the mind, or the heart?" Cyrus asked in his gentle baritone.

"Six of one and a half dozen of the other."

After a moment of silence Cyrus said, "I have a sympathetic ear, my boy, and a discreet tongue."

It was a curiously old-fashioned phrasing, but Ryder wasn't tempted to laugh. He stared into the dying fire and, even though it wasn't in his nature to confide his troubles, he felt the urge to talk.

"Have you ever wanted something so badly that you were terrified it would slip through your fingers?" he asked the older man slowly.

"Yes. You're talking about Amanda."

Ryder wasn't surprised by the statement. He knew he'd given himself away to nearly everyone in the house. Everyone except Amanda. "I'm afraid I pushed her too hard. She looked so . . . so white. So withdrawn. I'm afraid I sent her so far into her shell that

I won't be able to reach her again. That's why I'm sitting down here. Because I'm afraid to go upstairs and find out."

"I knew a young man once," Cyrus said softly, "who fell in love with a woman who bore scars. He wanted to heal her, to see her look at him with the trust that had been stolen from her. But what he didn't understand, what his love blinded him to, was the simple fact that the unshadowed trust he wanted from her no longer existed within her. Because he didn't understand that, he kept searching, probing. He believed that she had only to realize that *he* wouldn't hurt her for that trust to shine in her eyes."

"What happened?" Ryder asked when the old man's voice trailed away.

"He lost her. She was everything to him. He went to her heart—whole and untouched by pain. And being so flawless in his own love, he expected as much from her. She gave him all of herself—except that part of her forever lost. And that was the part he wanted so badly."

"But if they loved each other?"

"It should have been enough, shouldn't it? And perhaps it would have been, had things been different. You see, he didn't lose her because she couldn't give him what he wanted. He lost her because he thought his love was obvious—and it wasn't. She couldn't look at him with unshadowed trust, and so she never saw his love."

Ryder hesitated, then repeated slowly, "Unshadowed trust . . ."

"Unshadowed trust," Cyrus said gently, "is the

trust of a child. Not a woman. A child sees what is there and trusts blindly. But a woman has to hear the words before she believes."

The old man's story sank into Ryder's mind, and he felt a pang sharper than anything he'd ever felt before. Was that what he wanted from Amanda, unshadowed trust? Was that why he had remained silent about his own feelings even after he was certain of them? Because he wanted her to trust him so completely that she would willingly offer up everything she was to him?

Cinderella and a faith in princes.

He had battered at her detachment, seeing it for the defense it was, and yet *not* seeing it, not realizing that the kind of trust he wanted from her was gone. What trust she had to give would have to be won with patience and care.

And he had offered her nothing to believe in.

"I ought to be shot," he muttered, hardly aware of speaking aloud.

"Surely nothing so drastic," Cyrus murmured. He glanced at the younger man rather searchingly, and frowned a little.

Ryder started slightly as the sound of a muffled thump came from the general direction of the kitchen. "Damn furnace," he said. "I'll have to go kick it."

"Why don't you let me deal with that," Cyrus said casually. "I have a way with furnaces. You might want to take an extra blanket up to Amanda. She might get cold."

Ryder looked at him for a moment, then slowly smiled. "Yes, I think I should do that. Thank you, Cyrus."

The old man sat placidly on the couch and watched Ryder leave the room. He made no effort to rise and go attend to the temperamental furnace, but continued to sit tranquilly and gaze into the fire.

He wasn't at all surprised when the furnace started back up a few minutes later.

Ryder didn't stop to get an extra blanket. He went upstairs quickly to reach Amanda's bedroom door. He hesitated, then turned the knob silently and went into the room, closing the door behind him. The snow outside still provided considerable brightness, and he could make out her slender form in the bed. She was on the far side, turned toward the window with her back to him.

He listened for a few moments, suspending his own breathing in order to hear hers. It was deep and even, almost soundless. She was asleep, he knew. Without reaching the decision consciously, he began unbuttoning his shirt.

Amanda was vaguely aware of some indefinable difference, but she couldn't seem to wake up and find out what it was. She thought she felt a whisper of cool air, then a movement beneath her, and there was a warmth beside her that she was hazily delighted by.

"Beloved . . . beloved . . ."

She felt gentle hands touching her, turning her onto her back, and she lifted her arms instinctively to encircle his neck. A low, rough voice was still whispering to her, and warm lips touched her face with the lightness of a breath.

Dreaming. That was it. She was quite definitely dreaming. On the point of opening her eyes, Amanda chose to keep them firmly closed instead. She tilted her head to allow the warm lips access to her throat, murmuring a kittenlike purr of pleasure.

"You're so beautiful . . . Amanda . . ."

He was so gentle. Her nightgown was smoothed away tenderly, his hands stroking her body as if it were some precious jewel. His mouth caressed her with silky hunger. She began to burn, slowly, her nerve endings tingling, her blood heating, rushing through her veins. Her heartbeat seemed to spread throughout her body until she could feel it everywhere, a slow throbbing.

Eyes still tightly closed, she shifted restlessly, a pleading murmur escaping her lips. She felt him move, and eagerly cradled his body as he rose above her.

"Look at me, sweetheart," he whispered.

She was afraid the dream would vanish if she looked, but she couldn't ignore that husky command. Her eyes drifted open, and she saw him. The pale light provided by the snow outside lent his face an expression of stark tenderness she'd never seen before.

"Ryder," she murmured.

He lowered his head and kissed her, and her last doubt about this being real vanished like smoke. It was electrifying, overwhelming, consuming her. She moaned into his mouth like a wild thing trapped on the run, desperate, her arms tightening frantically around him as she felt the slow invasion of his body.

In the past, the intensity between them had grown quickly, a swift, unrelenting coiling of passion that never let up until it finally snapped. This time the dreamlike beginning had built desire slowly to a white-hot need that seared them both.

Amanda had never felt such pleasure, waves and waves of it, swamping her senses. She was hardly conscious of crying, of repeating his name over and over in a voice that was hardly there.

And when it was finally over, she was so utterly drained and peaceful that she could only cuddle close to the hard warmth of his body, secure in his arms, and tumble instantly into a deep, dreamless sleep.

Beloved.

Sweetheart?

She was just beginning to wake up. And, as always, it was a slow process. A friend had once talked about going to a dentist to have wisdom teeth extracted under an anesthetic; she'd said that the sensations had been so strange as she was waking up, that first she'd heard sounds, and then her mind had begun working, but her eyes had been the last thing to function properly.

Amanda had been mildly surprised. Not by the sensations, but by the fact that her friend had found them unusual. She'd thought everyone woke up that way.

So now, as usual, she was dimly aware of sound first. Breathing. Her mind started sluggishly to work, and she realized it wasn't her breathing. She gradually recaptured the misty thoughts that had followed her up from dreaming.

Beloved.

Sweetheart.

She had dreamed about Ryder. Slipping into bed with her in the middle of the night and making love to her. But . . . it hadn't been a dream, because he was with her now.

Amanda forced her eyes open. A blur, as usual. She fumbled one hand up to rub her eyes gently. Her other hand, she realized dimly, was trapped somewhere. Either under her or under him.

The dryness under her eyelids eased, and she blinked several times. Better.

"Awake?"

He was raised on an elbow beside her, one arm lying across her middle. She still couldn't figure out where her other arm was. It was still attached to her, presumably, but— She felt pins and needles, and gingerly worked the missing arm out from under the pillow. His pillow.

"Yes," she said cautiously. "I think."

"Good. I love you, Amanda."

# *Nine*

"What?" she said.

Ryder smiled, but his eyes remained very serious. "I said I love you."

She swallowed hard and tried to think. "This is very sudden, isn't it?"

"No. You may have noticed that I've been chasing after you like a madman."

Amanda stared up at him, feeling the sudden burning of tears and a wild surge of happiness. "You love me? Really?"

"I love you desperately." He bent his head and kissed her with all the tenderness she had thought she'd dreamed.

"Ryder," she said when she could, "you were right about me. I was so afraid to risk anything—"

"Wait." He rested his fingers gently, fleetingly, over her lips. "I want you to hear all of it."

She nodded, not wary but more than a little worried because he looked so grave. "All right."

The fingers that had covered her lips began to stroke her cheek lightly. His voice was low and steady. "When you fell off that ladder into my arms, I wanted you. It was so sudden it was like a bolt of lightning. I didn't even know your name, and, to tell the truth, I didn't care. Nothing like that had ever happened to me before, and I didn't quite trust it at first.

"You were beautiful and, heaven knows, desirable, but what I felt was so intense, it couldn't be rationally explained. So I stopped trying to explain it for a while. I just accepted it. I wanted you. So, naturally, I went after you." He smiled.

"I noticed," she murmured.

"Yes. Well, I suppose I thought that it would all make sense once we were lovers. But that's not what happened. The feelings just kept getting stronger. And I kept shying away from defining them."

Amanda was puzzled. "Why? Because you didn't want to fall in love?"

"No. Because I was convinced I *couldn't* be in love. Not with you." When she started to speak again, he shook his head. "Wait. Hear me out. I knew you'd been hurt, and I guessed that your . . . your detachment was a kind of defense, but it was driving me crazy that I couldn't get close to you except physically, and I couldn't explain to myself why I'd suddenly become so intense and possessive. I wanted to be important to you, to matter to you. I wanted you to trust me enough to be vulnerable with me, to share yourself with me."

"That sounds a lot like love to me," she said a bit unsteadily.

"It did to me too. When I stopped denying that, I

realized it was true. I was in love with you. It came as a shock because . . . the week before you and I met, I'd been obsessed with another woman."

Amanda went very still. "You were?"

"Yes. I couldn't understand how it was possible for me to feel so much for two different women. Then, the day before yesterday, I found you on another ladder. You said something totally innocent, and it clicked in my mind with another thing that had been nagging at me subconsciously. And it all made sense."

She was almost afraid to ask, her thoughts whirling in confusion. "Something I said? What did I say?"

"About the moosehead. You said something about it being rotten to hunt something that couldn't shoot back."

Amanda was still puzzled. "And the other thing?"

"Your perfume. You must wear a specially made blend; I've never noticed anything like it."

"My uncle had it made for me on my twenty-first birthday. I've worn it ever since. And it is my own blend. No one else is supposed to have it." For the first time, she thought she had an inkling of what he was talking about. But she couldn't believe it. It just didn't seem possible that he could have fallen in love with her *twice*.

"That's why I remembered it." Ryder sighed a bit roughly. "Amanda, if you'll go into my room and look on the shelf in the closet, you'll find a glass shoe. I don't know why I packed it. I don't even remember doing it. But I wasn't really surprised to unpack it here, since I'd been obsessed with it for more than a week. Or, rather, obsessed with the lady who had left it behind."

"Ryder—"

"I never consciously made the connection, because all I had to go on were my own feelings and a kind of subliminal awareness. She was blond and blue-eyed, her voice was a little huskier than yours. And she wore a mask. We were together in a dim garden, and for only a couple of hours. But I started falling in love with her that night. And then I came here, and fell in love with you. I won't ask you to try the shoe on, Amanda. We both know it would fit."

She reached up to touch his cheek with her fingertips. "I wasn't trying to deceive you, Ryder. I mean, not you specifically."

He smiled. "I know. One night to be Cinderella instead of Amanda Wilderman?"

She had to laugh, albeit weakly. "I lost a bet. My two cousins set the whole thing up. The costume, the shoes, the wig, and the limo. Everything. It was their present to me, because they thought I was getting cynical. A night to be anonymous, to believe in fairy tales."

"But you didn't believe in princes."

"No. Long ago I stopped expecting men to be princes. The whole time I kept telling myself how absurd it was. I even meant to take off the mask at midnight. But I couldn't. I was afraid that if you knew who I was, it would spoil everything. So I ran." She managed another laugh. "I never meant to drop that shoe, I swear. It just happened."

Ryder chuckled suddenly. "No wonder you were so appalled when I showed up here."

"I felt like a fool," she confessed in a small voice. "And then I had to tell you I was using Mother's name. I wasn't about to admit to having been Cinderella—especially since, for all I knew, you didn't even remember her."

"I remembered her. Oh, how I remembered her." He kissed her gently. "I had pushed her to the back of my mind because I was involved with you so quickly. But Amanda, I couldn't forget her. When I realized that she was you, I was delighted."

She heard something in his voice, a kind of restraint, and felt tension seep into her body.

Ryder felt the reaction, and his arm tightened across her middle as he smiled at her quickly. "I have to apologize to you, beloved."

The endearment sent such a rush of happiness through her that she almost forgot to ask. "For what?"

"The things I said to you yesterday. I wanted to get through to you, to make you respond to me emotionally, and I resorted to shock tactics. It was wrong, and cruel, and I'm sorry."

Amanda shook her head. "I think I needed to hear some of those things you said. It . . . it shook me up. I was being so careful to protect myself, to avoid pain—"

"No, Amanda, your reaction was the natural one. You'd been hurt. Of course you protected yourself. I was pushing too hard, expecting too much of you too quickly."

"I should have risked more. I—"

"It was too soon for you."

She gazed up at him, her eyes a little fierce, and said suddenly in a raw, shaking voice, "I love you. Ryder, I love you so much."

He caught her in his arms, lifting her against him, his face buried against the warmth of her neck. She could feel him shudder, as if some dreadful tension had snapped.

"Thank God," he muttered thickly. His eyes were burning silver as he raised his head to meet her gaze. "I was afraid you wouldn't be able to love me. Afraid you couldn't trust me enough not to hurt you."

Amanda smiled up at him with a glow in her eyes he'd never seen before. It wasn't, he knew, the unshadowed trust of a child. It was the trust of a woman who knew all the potential pain trust brings— and was willing to risk it.

"You shook me off that fence," she said softly. "You made me see that by hoarding the love I felt for you, by locking it away inside me, in the dark, I was hurting myself. I have to trust you. I love you too much to have a choice about it."

He kissed her, over and over, holding her tightly in his arms and murmuring love words in a fierce, hoarse voice. Her response was instant, fiery, and her own voice was shaken by the intensity of what she felt.

The force caught them, and for the first time neither of them held anything back.


It was late that afternoon when Amanda closed the front door and stood in the foyer holding a manila envelope. She tapped the edge of it against one hand thoughtfully. It was bulky, securely sealed, and in the upper left-hand corner bore the logo of Wilderman Electronics.

She knew what was sealed within, since she had discussed the details with both her uncle and the CEO of her company at considerable length the day before. And she knew as well that in terms of dollar value, Ryder couldn't possibly offer a better deal for the rights to the patent.

She knew, now, that whatever the outcome of this "fight," nothing would change between her and Ryder. She also knew that he would manage to build Foxxfire until it was competitive with her own company, because he was too honest and too ambitious to have it any other way.

And Amanda had expectations now. She thought that one day Foxxfire and Wilderman Electronics might possible merge, or join forces in some other way.

One day.

"A bit late, isn't it?" Ryder asked briskly as he came in. "You said early afternoon."

"The driver told me he got stuck behind a snow-plow." She looked at him with a tiny smile. "Is yours ready?"

"Yes. Up in that room that used to be mine. Cyrus says he'll have an answer for us by tomorrow morning."

She handed him her envelope. "Then you do the honors and take this up to him."

Ryder weighed it in his hand and lifted a brow at her. "The best deal you can offer?"

Amanda's smile widened. She felt secure enough in their love to be unworried by which of them would acquire the rights to Dunbar's patent. "You told me to fight. In that envelope is the offer we would have made Dunbar—and more. It's the best offer we could possibly make."

He bent his head to kiss her briefly. "Good."

"Does it really matter now?" she asked him curiously.

"Yes. I'm going to make a point. It's why I wanted you to fight me in the first place."

Mildly Amanda said, "It sounded like you wanted me to fight because you didn't want to win by default."

"That too."

"I thought pride was a sin."

"Not pride. Arrogance. You said so."

Amanda thought about that, then studied him speculatively. "You're very sure of yourself. I wonder why."

"Sweetheart, I can't lose." He kissed her again. "I've already got you."

"Yes, but—"

"Patience. I'm not ready to make my point yet. You'll just have to wait until Cyrus gives us his answer."

She had to be content with that. And was.

Since she and Ryder couldn't stay away from each other for more than ten minutes at a time, Amanda didn't get very much work done that day. She was already framing a mental apology to her uncle for abandoning the project halfway through, because she knew she'd return to Boston with Ryder.

She didn't think Uncle Ed would mind, particularly since she had a sneaking suspicion that he had offered her this job more to appease Samantha than out of desperate need. Whatever had happened to overset Sam's plans, she had obviously intended to get Ryder out here one way or another.

As far as Amanda was concerned, it had worked out fine.

She woke the next morning even later than usual—sort of. She had actually awakened fairly early, seduced from sleep by the scent of the coffee Ryder had brought her. Then she was seduced again, very thoroughly, and participated in her own seduction with such intensity that the aftermath became a sated, peaceful sleep.

When she woke the second time, she was alone in bed, which didn't surprise her. Ryder, she had discovered, had enough energy for three people, and although he channeled a considerable amount of that into lovemaking, there was always plenty left over.

She took a shower and got dressed, and was sitting on the bed brushing her hair when Ryder came in.

"Hello," he said, dropping two manila envelopes on the nightstand and then bending down to kiss her. The position was obviously unsatisfactory to him, because when Amanda became aware of her surroundings again, she found herself lying back on the bed with him smiling down at her.

"If," she said, "we could bottle that, we could both retire."

"Technology will never be able to bottle that," he said with conviction.

"Then we'll keep it our secret."

"Agreed. Now, shall we take care of business before we get down to pleasure?"

Amanda glanced toward the nightstand. "You've obviously seen Cyrus. He turned us both down?"

"No. He's gone, by the way. Said he had to get back, and to thank you for an enjoyable stay. And for your offer."

She blinked. "He accepted yours?"

"Uh-huh." Ryder was matter-of-fact.

Her first feeling was one of surprise, quickly replaced by satisfaction for Ryder's sake—and curiosity. "What did you offer him?"

He sat up and reached for one of the envelopes on the nightstand. Amanda pushed herself up as well, and accepted the sheaf of papers he handed her.

"See for yourself."

Amanda was no stranger to contracts, and swiftly located the relevant paragraphs. She read carefully, silently calculating that Ryder's offer would net Cyrus Fortune less than half of what her own company had promised. Then she read the final paragraph. She lifted a stunned gaze to Ryder. "I don't get it," she said somewhat weakly.

Leaning back on an elbow on the bed, Ryder said gravely, "In the course of casual conversation he mentioned that he'd always wanted a particular thing—and it isn't the kind of thing you buy—much less buy for yourself."

"You aren't going to—"

"No, of course not. I told you I didn't approve of that kind of thing. But I have a friend who wants to sell his."

She stared at him for a long moment, then began to giggle. "Wait until the members of the board find out what beat us."

Ryder grinned at her. "When you want something from somebody, the first thing you do is find out what *they* want. Then you can bargain."

"I'll remember that." She sobered, and leaned back on the bed to face him gravely. "And your point?"

He nodded. "Why I wanted you to fight for the deal. You avoided expectations because you didn't want to be disappointed. With this deal you couldn't help but expect to win; it was the only rational way to look at it, since you knew damned well you could outbid me."

"Yes. And so?"

He reached out to touch her cheek gently. "My point is that winning is never certain. And losing is never certain. But you should always *expect* to win. You should always have a goal worth fighting for."

Amanda smiled slowly. "I love you, you know."

He pulled her over into his arms. "I love you too, Cinderella. But with the best will in the world, I can't be a prince."

"Can't you?" she murmured, tracing the outline of his lips with one fingertip.

His arms tightened around her, and his eyes burned silver. "Tell me how, sweetheart."

She held her voice steady. "Princes . . . fulfill expectations. I have only one."

Ryder gazed up into her heartbreaking green eyes for a long moment. "I want to spend the rest of my life with you," he said simply. "Marry me, Amanda."

Her smile grew, lighting her eyes with a glow of sheer happiness. "That was it," she whispered.

"Manda—" Samantha stared down at the dog and nudged his limp form with one cautious foot. "What on earth is wrong with him?"

"You startled him bursting through the door like that," Amanda told her. "He was already tense from the flight out here, and very nervous. He fainted."

"Fainted?"

"He'll be all right in a minute." Nemo was, in fact, already stirring.

Samantha shook her head as one who refused to ponder unfathomable things. "Oh."

"What was the rush anyway?" her father asked, looking up from his breakfast.

Sam went around the table to her place and slid into her chair. She looked across at Amanda and Ryder who, along with Edward Wilderman, had been enjoying a peaceful morning meal. "Well . . ."

"Give," Amanda invited firmly.

"Oh, it was just that I thought it'd be perfect, and I can't imagine what on earth happened to it. I mean, I didn't think about it last night when you two got here because you were married already and it was so exciting." Almost immediately she added in an aggrieved tone. "Though I *still* think a big church wedding—"

"Samantha, I love you dearly, but the thought of giving you a chance to arrange a wedding filled me with profound misgivings." Amanda winced.

Sam's green eyes were innocent. "But why? Such a perfect ending to the story. So romantic. You in your costume and Ryder in his. Both of you with crowns. And a huge church with a long aisle like in *The Sound of Music*. It would have been so great."

Ryder looked at his new wife and grinned. "Now I understand what you warned me about."

Amanda nodded. "I knew you had only to meet Samantha to appreciate her."

"Hey, guys," Sam said mildly, "I'm still here."

"We know," Edward murmured. "And you didn't

answer the original question, Sam. What was the rush?"

Leslie, entering the dining room just then in a hurry but without the violently banging door that had so startled poor Nemo, immediately demanded of her sister, "Did you tell them yet?"

"She was about to," their father said patiently. "Sit down, Les. Sam?"

Samantha looked at Ryder. "After Manda dropped the shoe that night, did you get it? And keep it?"

"Yes."

She sighed. "Well, at least you'll have one of them, then. I was hoping . . . But it'll be a terrific memento of the night you met. You can put it on a cushion under glass or something. A great conversation piece."

Amanda and Ryder exchanged glances and then, in mutual silent agreement, looked at Edward Wilderman.

"This time," he said, "she's lost me."

Samantha looked mildly frustrated. "You people are terribly dense this morning."

Helping herself to bacon from a tray on the table, Leslie said, "Some stories can be told from the middle, because everybody knows how they start. But if they *don't* know, you should start at the beginning."

Sam looked at her, then at the others. With exquisite clarity she said, "It's gone."

"*What's* gone?" Amanda asked.

"The other shoe."

"Sam, I've got the other shoe."

Samantha smiled suddenly. "You took it with you after all? Oh, good. Now you'll have both of—"

"Samantha." Amanda was beginning to realize there was something peculiar here. "You know you put that shoe in my suitcase when I wasn't looking."

"I did not," Sam denied instantly. "Hey, I took you at your word in the limo when you said you never wanted to set eyes on it again. When we got home, I shoved it into the back of my closet. I didn't know it was gone until just now."

After a moment Edward said reflectively. "She's very truthful, you know. If she says she didn't—"

"I didn't," Sam repeated flatly.

Amanda looked, more or less automatically, at Leslie, who immediately disclaimed any responsibility.

"Not me. Sam's the brains of this outfit. Whenever one of her plans is unfolding, I keep my fingers out of it."

"Which is as it should be," Sam told her.

Leslie looked at her orange juice and said meditatively, "Which is safer."

Amanda looked at Ryder. "Then how on earth? I didn't put it there. I never saw it after the ball until I got out to the ranch and unpacked."

Samantha grinned at them both. "Sort of makes you believe in fate, doesn't it?"

# *Epilogue*

He closed the file with a satisfied smile and put it to one side on the big desk. He tapped one finger against the thick manila envelope lying on the other side of the desk and mused aloud. "There'll be a great deal of money from this, unless I'm mistaken."

"You never are," she said.

He chuckled, a deep, rich sound. "Thank you, sweet. But the problem remains. A university, perhaps?"

"Scholarships. There are never enough to go around."

"Good, good," he murmured, nodding. "And as for the other little matter—"

"No," she said.

His dark eyes gleamed with mischief. "Well, but I could hang it in here."

"I will not," she said, "have a murdered animal hanging on a wall in my house, Cyrus."

He chuckled again. "I wish I could have seen her face," he said wistfully. "Still, I suppose you're right, my love. I'll have it sent . . . somewhere."

He reached out to the tidy stack of files and lifted the topmost one, opening it on the desk before him. In the golden circle of light provided by a shaded lamp he studied the papers in the file thoughtfully.

"This is the one you've waited for, isn't it?" She had risen from her chair and come to him, standing by his chair and resting one small hand on his shoulder.

He reached up to clasp it with the extreme gentleness of a very large and powerful man. "Yes. For thirty-five years."

"It wasn't your fault, Cy."

"If I had arrived on time . . ."

"You were delayed. And perhaps that was the way it had to be. How often have I heard you say that everything happens in its own time?"

After a moment he looked up at her and smiled. "All right, sweet. Point taken. But the time is now—and I won't be delayed."

"How long do you have?"

He studied the file. "The events have already been set in motion; there's no stopping them. At best I'll have until Christmas."

**Be sure to watch for the next delightful romance in Kay Hooper's "Once Upon a Time . . ." series.**

# THE EDITOR'S CORNER

This month our color reflects the copper leaves of autumn, and we hope when a chill wind blows, you'll curl up with a LOVESWEPT. In keeping with the seasons, next month our color will be the deep green of a Christmas pine, and our books will carry a personalized holiday message from the authors. You'll want to collect all six books just because they're beautiful—but the stories are so wonderful, even wrapped in plain brown paper they'd be appealing!

Sandra Brown is a phenomenon! She never disappoints us. In **A WHOLE NEW LIGHT,** LOVESWEPT #366, Sandra brings together two special people. Cyn McCall desperately wants to shake up her life, but when Worth Lansing asks her to spend the weekend with him in Acapulco, she's more than a little surprised—and tempted. Worth had always been her buddy, her friend, her late husband's business partner. But what will happen when Cyn sees him in a whole new light?

Linda Cajio's gift to you is a steamy, sensual romance: **UNFORGETTABLE,** LOVESWEPT #367. Anne Kitteridge and James Farraday also know each other. In fact, they've known each other all their lives. Anne can't forget how she'd once made a fool of herself over James. And James finds himself drawn once again to the woman who was his obsession. When James stables his prize horse at Anne's breeding farm, they come together under the most disturbingly intimate conditions, and there's no way they can deny their feelings. As always Linda creates an emotionally charged atmosphere in this unforgettable romance.

*(continued)*

Courtney Henke's first LOVESWEPT, **CHA-MELEON,** was charming, evocative, and tenderly written, and her second, **THE DRAGON'S REVENGE,** LOVESWEPT #368 is even more so. J.D. Smith is instantly captivated by Charly, the woman he sees coaching a football team of tough youths, and he wonders what it would be like to tangle with the woman her players call the Dragon Lady. He's met his match in Charly—in more ways than one. When he teaches her to fence, they add new meaning to the word touché.

Joan Elliott Pickart will cast a spell over you with **THE MAGIC OF THE MOON,** LOVESWEPT #369. She brings together Declan Harris, a stressed-out architect, and Joy Barlow, a psychologist, under the rare, romantic light of a blue moon—and love takes over. Declan cherishes Joy, but above all else she wants his respect—the one thing he finds hardest to give. Joan comes through once more with a winning romance.

LOVESWEPT #370, **POOR EMILY** by Mary Kay McComas is not to be missed. The one scene sure to make you laugh out loud is when Emily's cousin explains to her how finding a man is like choosing wallpaper. It's a scream! Mary Kay has a special touch when it comes to creating two characters who are meant to be together. Emily falls for Noble, the hero, even before she meets him, by watching him jog by her house every day. But when they do meet, Emily and Noble find they have lots more in common than ancestors who fought in the Civil War—and no one ever calls her Poor Emily again.

Helen Mittermeyer begins her *Men of Ice* series
*(continued)*

with **QUICKSILVER**, LOVESWEPT #371. Helen is known for writing about strong, dangerous, enigmatic men, and hero Piers Larraby is all of those things. When gorgeous, silver-haired Damiene Belson appears from the darkness fleeing her pursuers, Piers is her sanctuary in the storm. But too many secrets threaten their unexpected love. You can count on Helen to deliver a dramatic story filled with romance.

Don't forget to start your holiday shopping early this year. Our LOVESWEPT Golden Classics featuring our Hometown Hunk winners are out in stores right now, and in the beginning of November you can pick up our lovely December LOVE-SWEPTs. They make great gifts. What could be more joyful than bringing a little romance into someone's life?

Best wishes,
Sincerely,

*Carolyn Nichols*

Carolyn Nichols
  Editor
*LOVESWEPT*
Bantam Books
666 Fifth Avenue
New York, NY 10103

# FAN OF THE MONTH

**Tricia Smith**

I'm honored to have been chosen as a "fan of the month" for LOVESWEPT. A mother of two children with a house full of animals, I've been a romance reader for years. I was immediately captivated when I read the first LOVESWEPT book, **HEAVEN'S PRICE** by Sandra Brown. Ms. Brown is a very compelling author, along with so many of the authors LOVESWEPT has introduced into my life.

Each month I find myself looking forward to new adventures in reading with LOVESWEPT. The story lines are up-to-date, very well researched, and totally enthralling. With such fantastic authors as Iris Johansen, Kay Hooper, Fayrene Preston, Kathleen Creighton, Joan Elliott Pickart, and Deborah Smith, I'm always enchanted, from cover to cover, month after month.

I recently joined the Gold Coast Chapter of Romance Writers of America and have made wonderful friends who are all well-known authors as well as just great people. I hope to attend an RWA convention someday soon in order to meet the authors who've enriched my life in so many ways. Romance reading for me is not a pasttime but a passion.

# 60 Minutes to a Better, More Beautiful You!

**N** ow it's easier than ever to awaken your sensuality, stay slim forever—even make yourself irresistible. With Bantam's bestselling subliminal audio tapes, you're only 60 minutes away from a better, more beautiful you!

| | | |
|---|---|---|
| __ 45004-2 | **Slim Forever** | $8.95 |
| __ 45112-X | **Awaken Your Sensuality** | $7.95 |
| __ 45081-6 | **You're Irresistible** | $7.95 |
| __ 45035-2 | **Stop Smoking Forever** | $8.95 |
| __ 45130-8 | **Develop Your Intuition** | $7.95 |
| __ 45022-0 | **Positively Change Your Life** | $8.95 |
| __ 45154-5 | **Get What You Want** | $7.95 |
| __ 45041-7 | **Stress Free Forever** | $7.95 |
| __ 45106-5 | **Get a Good Night's Sleep** | $7.95 |
| __ 45094-8 | **Improve Your Concentration** | $7.95 |
| __ 45172-3 | **Develop A Perfect Memory** | $8.95 |

**Bantam Books, Dept. LT, 414 East Golf Road, Des Plaines, IL 60016**

Please send me the items I have checked above. I am enclosing $_____
(please add $2.00 to cover postage and handling). Send check or money
order, no cash or C.O.D.s please. (Tape offer good in USA only.)

Mr/Ms _____

Address _____

City/State _____ Zip _____

LT-12/89

Please allow four to six weeks for delivery.
Prices and availability subject to change without notice.

# THE DELANEY DYNASTY

Men and women whose loves an passions are so glorious
it takes many great romance novels by three bestselling
authors to tell their tempestuous stories.

## THE SHAMROCK TRINITY

| | | | |
|---|---|---|---|
| ☐ | 21975 | RAFE, THE MAVERICK<br>*by Kay Hooper* | $2.95 |
| ☐ | 21976 | YORK, THE RENEGADE<br>*by Iris Johansen* | $2.95 |
| ☐ | 21977 | BURKE, THE KINGPIN<br>*by Fayrene Preston* | $2.95 |

## THE DELANEYS OF KILLAROO

| | | | |
|---|---|---|---|
| ☐ | 21872 | ADELAIDE, THE ENCHANTRESS<br>*by Kay Hooper* | $2.75 |
| ☐ | 21873 | MATILDA, THE ADVENTURESS<br>*by Iris Johansen* | $2.75 |
| ☐ | 21874 | SYDNEY, THE TEMPTRESS<br>*by Fayrene Preston* | $2.75 |

## THE DELANEYS: *The Untamed Years*

| | | | |
|---|---|---|---|
| ☐ | 21899 | GOLDEN FLAMES *by Kay Hooper* | $3.50 |
| ☐ | 21898 | WILD SILVER *by Iris Johansen* | $3.50 |
| ☐ | 21897 | COPPER FIRE *by Fayrene Preston* | $3.50 |

**Buy them at your local bookstore or use this page to order.**

Bantam Books, Dept. SW7, 414 East Golf Road, Des Plaines, IL 60016

Please send me the items I have checked above. I am enclosing $_____
(please add $2.00 to cover postage and handling). Send check or money
order, no cash or C.O.D.s please.

Mr/Ms _____

Address _____

City/State _____ Zip _____

Please allow four to six weeks for delivery.                    SW7–11/89
Prices and availability subject to change without notice.